HOW TO TRAIN A COWBOY

BY
CARO CARSON

HarperCollins
PUBLISHERS
Since 1817

First Published in Great Britain 2017
By Mills & Boon, an imprint of HarperCollins*Publishers*
1 London Bridge Street, London, SE1 9GF

© 2017 Caro Carson

ISBN: 978-0-263-92324-7

23-0817

Our policy is to use papers that are natural, renewable and recyclable
products and made from wood grown in sustainable forests. The logging and
manufacturing processes conform to the legal environmental regulations of
the country of origin.

Printed and bound in Spain
by CPI, Barcelona

Despite a no-nonsense background as a West Point graduate, army officer and Fortune 100 sales executive, **Caro Carson** has always treasured the happily-ever-after of a good romance novel. As a RITA® Award-winning Mills & Boon author, Caro is delighted to be living her own happily-ever-after with her husband and two children in Florida, a location which has saved the coaster-loving theme-park fanatic a fortune on plane tickets.

This book is dedicated to
my fellow Harlequin Special Edition authors.

Thank you for being the colleagues who understand
me, the friends I love to spend time with and the
authors who write the stories I love to read.

Chapter One

January 2015

He didn't belong here, either.

Graham pushed his empty beer glass toward the bartender and abandoned his bar stool. He hadn't belonged anywhere in a good, long while. He should have known a honky-tonk bar in Texas would be no different.

He'd been seduced by the appearance of this bar, he supposed. Something about the way it stood alone on the side of a rural road had caught his eye. The cinder block building was just old enough to prove the bar knew what it took to satisfy its customers, new enough to flaunt a pre-fab extension, all wood and aluminum. If it hadn't been the look of the building, then Graham would have stopped because the size of the dirt parking lot meant that the place must see enough business to keep its kegs fresh, even if the parking lot and the bar inside had been nearly empty as twilight set in. He hadn't expected such a fresh-faced crowd to start filling up the place so quickly after dark, though.

He should have. It was only Thursday, but the University of Texas in Austin was an hour east of here, and the massive army base, Fort Hood, an hour north. The average age inside the bar couldn't be more than twenty-one, even though it wasn't yet the weekend. Students and soldiers laughed and drank and tried to shout over a band that played Southern rock far too loudly for the low-ceilinged space.

No, Graham didn't belong here.

Eighteen months ago—a lifetime ago—he'd been Captain Benjamin Graham of the United States Marine Corps. For eight years, he'd served everywhere he was needed, from Japan to Europe, but after his last deployment to Afghanistan, he'd had the distinct feeling he no longer belonged in the military. His body had taken a beating in those years. The daily wear and tear of backpacks and boots had taken as much of a toll as the bursts of adrenaline that kept a Marine from noticing that he was bleeding while returning enemy fire.

But it was more than that.

Graham had simply known, one average day on an average rifle range while safely stateside, that he was done. He'd proven whatever it was young men had to prove when they volunteered for the service. He'd served his nation and he'd served with good people—but it was time to move on. Graham had submitted the proper paperwork to his chain of command. In short order, he'd gotten his final orders and left.

Those eight years felt like eighty, sometimes. Like now. Graham worked his way toward the exit, leading with his good shoulder as he snaked his way through the impossibly young crowd. He might have felt like the oldest thing around, but he knew he wasn't. The three-man band kept riffing—endlessly—on a Lynyrd Skynyrd tune that was older than he was. There were clusters of weathered men here and there, men like his uncle, who'd lived most of his sixty years outdoors, working a ranch.

The man ahead of him abruptly cut out of the traffic flow to join a group wearing black motorcycle jackets that matched. The biker lowered himself onto a bar stool as if his whole body ached, a feeling Graham knew too well. But the biker had gray in his beard; Graham was thirty. Maybe Graham had seen too much overseas to have any-thing in common with the young college crowd, but surely he didn't belong on a bar stool next to that biker. Not yet.

A woman stumbled into him, one of the college set.

He caught her with one hand as she glared over her shoulder at the girls who had pushed her into his path. Then she turned her attention to him with a flip of her hair. She bit her lip and checked him out from his eyes all the way low to the zipper of his jeans.

"Sorry," she said over the music, with a smile that said she wasn't sorry at all. Her top was cut low, her breasts were pushed high and she nudged against him as the crowd pushed them together.

Graham assumed the attention meant he must not look as old as he felt—which changed nothing.

"No problem." With an attempt at a polite smile, he turned sideways and stepped around her, leading now with the shoulder he'd shattered on the other side of the world. The shrieks of her girlfriends followed him. *He was so not into you* carried over the music, and was gone.

Graham soldiered on. The traffic flow was hampered by the pool table and a foosball game. He spotted another motor-cycle jacket, but it sported a different logo than the bearded man's club. Bikers, college kids, soldiers and locals—too many people in too small a space, with alcohol thrown into the mix. By the time that mix went sour, Graham would be long gone, but since everyone was peaceful for the moment, he changed his target from the exit door to a side hallway that held the restrooms. He didn't know how far he had left to drive tonight, maybe sixty miles. Best to hit the head while he could.

There was a line for the bathroom, but at least the hallway was marginally quieter, since it was out of the direct blast of the band's oversized speakers. Conversation continued all around him as he took his place in line with the men. Women formed a line on the opposite wall, the sexes as segregated as they'd be at a dance in a middle school gym. Each time a person came out of either of the bathrooms, bright light and the sound of running water spilled into the little hallway.

Graham resisted the reflex of closing one eye at each burst of bright light. This wasn't a combat zone. He didn't need to save the night vision in one eye each time the enemy sent up a flare. He let the back of his head rest on the wall and closed both eyes, weary of his own habitual alertness.

"Come on. Just one drink. I'm buying." A male voice, cajoling.

"No, thanks." A female voice, polite.

"Don't be like that. You're too pretty to pay for your own drinks."

Spare me from college hormones.

Graham had turned thirty this fall on a college campus while in pursuit of an MBA. Although he'd realized pretty quickly that going back to graduate school wasn't right for him, he'd forced himself to finish the semester. Most of his fellow students had entered straight from their bachelor's degree programs, which meant they were twenty-one-year-olds like this guy, who was green enough to try to seduce a girl who needed to use a bathroom.

Graham had quit the MBA program a few weeks ago, at the end of the semester. The university had a nicer name for it; they'd charitably listed him as *on sabbatical,* but Graham doubted he'd return. He didn't belong there, with the college boys.

"Come on," this college boy said. "Dance with me."

She doesn't want to dance if she's got to pee, pal.

If being thirty meant one had lived long enough to gain a few scars, it also meant one had gained some practical wisdom—or at least better control over one's hormones. Either way, he was grateful that he wasn't desperate enough to pursue a woman in a bathroom line. Graham opened his eyes and took the burst of bright light as the door opened.

"You gotta forgive me sooner or later," the young man said, managing to whine and laugh at the same time. "Come on, let me see that pretty smile. You want to smile for me, Em, I know you do."

Graham glanced at the man: button-down shirt, blond hair, tanned skin that said he'd probably spent the Christmas holidays somewhere tropical. The look on his face wasn't confidence but cockiness.

The woman whom the man seemed to think owed him a smile had her back to Graham. He let his gaze follow her dark brown hair as it flowed over the large, loose ruffles of her light blue dress, stray curls detouring on their own little paths here and there. Her hair fell all the way to the small of her back, capturing what light there was along the way, lustrous with youth and health.

The door shut, leaving them all in the dark.

Em, the man had called her. They knew one another.

"Why don't you go back to Mike and Doug?" This *Em* spoke almost like a teacher, not shrill, no giggles—a teacher whose patience was being tested as she tried to redirect a student's attention to something more appropriate. "I'll stop by in a minute and say hi. You don't want to stand in line here with me."

"I'm not leaving until you say yes." The man leaned in closer. "Come on. Say it. One little yes. You won't regret it."

Graham felt older than ever. Had he ever been that cocky? At what age did a man learn that persistence was annoying, not charming?

Then the ladies' room door opened again, the woman turned away from the college guy, and in the sudden bright light, Graham saw her face.

For one moment in time, just one suspended moment, Graham stopped thinking. The Marines, the bar, the MBA, everywhere he'd been, everywhere he was going, *everything* just ceased for a moment of blessed…interest. He looked at her, and he wanted to know her.

She was beautiful. Of course she was, but there was something about her, something that appealed beyond an oval face and pink lips and the smooth skin of a young woman, something in her expression—it felt like morning, to see her face in the bright light. For the first time in years, something, some*one* in the world, was interesting.

Their eyes met and held for a fraction of time, but then she blinked and turned back to the man who stood too close to her.

The guy poked the corner of her mouth with one finger. "Smile for me, baby."

She stepped backward.

Graham stepped forward.

Her back was to him, so he doubted she knew he was

standing behind her like some kind of bodyguard, but he stayed where he was. She didn't want to be touched by that guy. The way she'd jerked out of his reach made that obvious. She didn't even want to talk to the guy, but she was being too polite about it.

Women were too polite too often, something Graham had realized after playing wingman to an endless number of Marine buddies over the years. The awkward chuckle, the gentle *no, thank you*, the drink or the dance they ended up accepting although they didn't really want it at all—these were common ways women dealt with unwanted attention.

They shouldn't have to. How old did a woman have to be before she skipped right to telling a persistent creep to go to hell?

"Go to hell," said the woman in ruffles.

Graham looked at the back of her head and almost smiled.

The college guy looked surprised. "Don't be like that, Em. You've gotten all uptight, haven't you, without getting any—"

"Go to hell." She didn't raise her voice. "We're through. We've been through. We're always going to be through. I don't want to drink, and I don't want to dance. Leave me alone."

She turned her back on the guy, but since she hadn't known Graham was so close behind her, she nearly collided with him, her cheek grazing past his chin.

"Oh, sorry." Her apology was automatic, a reflex.

He put a hand out to steady her, also reflexively. But over her head, he locked gazes with the other guy deliberately.

"I heard her," Graham said. "Didn't you?"

The guy glanced at the way Graham kept his hand on

her arm, and he hesitated—his first smart move. For all the guy's youth, he was still a grown man, only an inch shorter than Graham, but there was nothing he could do that Graham could not counter, bad shoulder or not. That wasn't cockiness; that was confidence, earned the hard way, year after year in the Marine Corps.

Think about it, pal, before you put another finger on her.

Graham waited, hand lightly resting on her soft skin so he could get her out of the way if push came to shove.

Another opening of the door, another burst of light. The woman called Em nodded politely at Graham and stepped around him, her ruffles and soft hair whispering past his shoulder. Then she was gone inside, disappearing along with the light as the door slammed shut.

The woman who'd exited the ladies' room drawled an approving *hello* in the dark as she rubbed her way past Graham to head back into the crowd. His night vision was shot, but he didn't need it to know the college guy had made the smart choice and beat a retreat.

Which left Graham alone. Again.

He was next in the men's line, but when the door opened, he almost turned to let the next man have his place. Graham didn't want to miss her when she came back out.

Her. *Em.*

Just as quickly as he recognized that anticipation, that almost hopeful desire to see her again, he pounded it down. *Hopeful.* Who did he think he was?

She was self-possessed, confident—intriguing to him. But she was still young, a woman who'd calmly set her boundaries while wrapped in youthful blue ruffles.

He was nothing more than a jarhead who'd left the Marine Corps, who'd spent a year after that burning a few bridges in the corporate world, who'd returned to grad school only to drop out weeks ago. He was on his way to take the only job offer he had left, one from his uncle, one that would barely pay minimum wage, but one that would require little to no human contact in the rural part of Texas. He'd given up on fitting in with the world, and he had no business forgetting that tonight, not even for a minute.

Let the beauty live her beautiful life.

He stalked toward the blinding light, straight into the toilet stall, and slammed the door.

Oh, my gosh. Ohmigosh, ohmigosh—who was that man?

Emily washed her hands quickly, thoughts racing.

Heart racing.

She wasn't sure what had just happened. She'd taken one look at him and *bam!* Her heart had started pounding. Then when she'd turned around and brushed against his body, she'd practically melted at his feet. He was hot. Hot in a way that the other men in her world weren't.

She had the impression he could be dangerous, but she couldn't say why. He'd just stood there, really. Just said one sentence to her idiot ex and nothing to her at all. But there was an aura about him that left her in no doubt that he was a man with whom one did not mess. An aura and a hard body.

She shivered as her soapy fingers slid together, but it was a delicious shiver. None of that danger had been directed her way, but she'd felt it. And it had triggered just about every primitive response she was capable of. More than she'd known she was capable of. She'd never met a man like that, not on her college campus, not even among the cowboys on her family's ranch. She'd grown up here in cattle country, so she knew plenty of men who were plenty masculine, but none had ever been so…dangerous.

No, he wasn't dangerous to her. What was the word she was looking for?

Sexual.

Maybe it was just sexy to have a man step in to defend her.

Him, Tarzan. Me…Jane?

No way. As long as Emily could remember, she'd always been able to rope and ride and keep up with the boys in her life. Unlike poor helpless Jane, Emily would never stand still in a frilly dress and scream uselessly, waiting for a man to swoop out of the jungle to save her.

Maybe that's why no man ever has before.

She hadn't known she could feel like Jane, body set all aflutter because a physically powerful man had brushed against her dress. Emily barely dried her hands before using the paper towel to yank the door open.

Too eagerly.

Slow down.

Had she learned nothing in her twenty-two years? Had her sisters' dramatic love lives taught her nothing? Her mother's three marriages?

Slow down.

She, Emily Dawn Davis, was not going to have her life derailed by a man. She was no Victorian miss, no helpless paragon of femininity waiting for a man to complete her. In fact, she'd prefer not to have a man in her life at all right now. She had plans. Things to do. Places to be. Goals to accomplish.

But not tonight.

She was going to have to obey her family and return to Oklahoma Tech University in three days whether she stayed at this bar another three minutes or three hours. She'd intended to leave when she'd realized her ex was here at Keller's and her friends were not, but now…

A dangerous man had appointed himself her body-guard. For once, she understood the appeal in having a man take care of everything. What would life be like as Jane, not having to stand up for herself as long as Tarzan was around? She could just look pretty in her new blue dress and—and—

And not be in charge of my own life.

Her mother was controlling enough. Her older sisters, too. This entire winter break had been one frustration after another as they put roadblocks in her path. The last thing she needed was a man to give her his opinions on where to go and how to live.

It was time to leave. There was nothing she needed from a man, not even from a bodyguard.

The men's room door opened, and Tarzan stepped out in a blaze of light.

Sex.

Well. There was that.

She took in all the vivid details as the door slowly swung shut behind him. He wore a navy blue knit shirt, long sleeves pushed up his forearms. Snug jeans, not new. Boots, but not cowboy boots. Maybe he was a biker? His dark hair was just a shade shorter than most of the guys. Maybe he was from Fort Hood. A soldier?

She wanted to know. She was wild to know more about him.

In the last sliver of light before the door shut, their eyes met. The man had honest-to-goodness green eyes, a warm green, like the grass in autumn when she went riding, happy in her world.

Emily stared at him, mute. Had Jane been struck speechless when she'd first laid eyes on her uncivilized man?

We don't do helpless. Snap out of it.

Emily forced herself to move. She stuck out her hand

to shake his, as if she were back at the James Hill Ranch, meeting a new cowboy whom the foreman had hired for the season. Not the most feminine move, but it was better than staring.

"Hi there. I'm Emily Davis."

"Graham." He took her hand in his without taking his gaze off her face. He looked so terribly serious about a handshake, as if they were closing a business deal.

It occurred to her that she was accosting someone in a bathroom hallway, just like her ex had done. Just *ugh*. She was classier than this. More mature than this. Really, she was. But that electricity she'd felt when she'd first brushed against Tarzan was all there, that thrill in the air as warm palm met warm palm. Every crude line her girlfriends used to describe a sexy man, every purr about a man who could make a woman want to drop her panties at one smoldering look, all of them suddenly made sense.

Even his hand feels sexy.

He let go, gave her the slightest of nods and the smallest attempt at a smile, and then he started to shoulder past her.

No! Don't go. In sudden desperation, words popped out of her mouth, the oldest pick-up line in the world, the one dozens of men had used on her. With a jerk of her chin toward the bar, she raised her voice over the music and the crowd.

"Can I buy you a drink?"

Chapter Two

Ohmigosh, he said yes. I don't know what to do.

Yes, you do. Get your act together.

She was going to buy a man a drink. She'd asked, he'd nodded and it was as simple as that. She was no helpless Jane. She was Emily Davis, future rancher—whether her family approved of that goal or not—and current purchaser of a beer for a man whom she wanted to... Well, never mind where her mind went at the sight of him. She just wanted to be around him. So she was going to buy him a drink.

He'd gestured out of the hallway with his nod, so she'd turned and started pushing her way back into the crowd. Guitars and drums obliterated all but the loudest shouts as Emily headed for the far side of the room, where the iron-trimmed wooden bar stretched the length of the wall. The hottest man in her world was currently half behind her, half beside her, matching her every move as she dodged left and right around people who were talking and drinking and standing in one place. The rush was as exciting as that first drop on a roller coaster.

Emily wedged herself in between two other people at the bar. Like all the other girls who wanted the bartender's attention, Emily put her elbows on the iron-trimmed wood and started to lean forward, prepared to flirt her way into getting some service, but she felt Graham's presence behind her, and she paused. He was in a different league than her college crowd—the college she was being forced to return to. She didn't want to act like the other girls.

It wouldn't work, anyway. Leaning over the bar generally gave the bartender a nice cleavage shot, which would hopefully get his attention, but Emily's outfit was more subtle than that. Sure, her dress barely reached to mid-thigh and she was wearing her fancy cowboy boots, the ones that were only good for dancing, but her chest was covered with ruffles up to her neck, not exposed by a low neckline. Besides, the bartender tonight was Jason, helping out his family on his own winter break from college. She'd known Jason in high school, when her previous step-father had lived far outside of Austin and the school bus ride had taken over an hour each way. If the sight of Emily's cleavage was going to make Jason hustle over to her, it would have done so years ago.

"Yo, Jason!" But her shout had to compete with the band's cover of a Merle Haggard outlaw country tune. She whistled instead, another masculine move, but the piercing sound worked. Jason pointed at her to let her know he was coming her way next. She turned to ask Tarzan—Graham—what he'd like, but he wasn't paying attention to her. Instead, with his eyes narrowed and his jaw set, he was scanning the crowd.

Maybe he was looking for whichever friends he'd come in with. She hoped he wasn't looking for a particular girl, but that was entirely possible. He was undeniably handsome, and the protective streak he seemed to have—and the buff body his shirt clung to—only made him more appealing. Women would fall all over him, as she had.

He was watching someone in particular now, no longer scanning. The thrill she'd felt from having his attention dropped a notch.

"Is beer okay?" she asked over the band.

He didn't hear her.

She reached out to touch him, her fingertips sliding over his shirtsleeve, the curve of his bicep solid underneath that soft knit.

He looked at her.

"Light beer?" she asked, pointing at the handles of the beer taps in case he couldn't hear her. "Dark beer?"

He shook his head and made a small gesture with his hand, almost like he was busy and she shouldn't bother him. *Nothing. Not right now.*

Disappointment flooded through her, washing the thrill away. A little embarrassment heated her cheeks, because she'd misread him. That nod in the bathroom hallway hadn't meant *Yes, I'd like to spend more time with you,* after all. He probably hadn't even heard her question in the first place. He'd just been on his way to the bar himself. He was waiting for her to get her drink and go back to her friends, so he could order his and go back to whomever he was looking for.

There was nothing more Emily could do. Graham had turned half away from her again. Since he wasn't even looking at her, she could hardly flirt with him now, even if she had the guts to risk a second rejection.

Emily caught Jason's eye and held up one finger. *One beer, darn it. One lonely beer.*

From somewhere beyond the pool table, a male voice

shouted in anger. Two voices. More. Suddenly, Graham's hand was on her waist, his palm immediately warm through the thin blue material of her dress. Emily turned to him in surprise just as a flurry of violence erupted near the pool table.

The crowd lurched away as one, pushing everyone a foot closer to the bar, butting up against Graham. He was braced for it, though, and didn't move. Emily wasn't squashed at all, not with him standing like a wall, breaking the tide of people coming at her.

Emily stepped back as much as she could to give him room, but she could only back up a half step until the rounded iron edge of the bar touched her back. He stepped with her, keeping his hand on her waist, then placed his other hand on the bar beside her and braced his arm straight. There was more shouting, another surge as people tried to get out of the way of the fistfight. Emily was sheltered from the second wave, too, safe as she looked up into those green eyes, feeling Graham's muscles flex as he kept his arm stiff and people collided with his back, and *wow, this is much too sexy*.

She could love being Jane. It would be too easy to get addicted to having this man protect her from the dangers of the jungle.

But he shouldn't have to. The crowd pushed against him, and Emily grimaced apologetically. Fistfights around here were usually over as soon as they started, but the distinctive sound of a pool cue cracking cut through the air, as loud as a baseball bat splintering on a fast pitch. Women screamed.

"Let's go," Graham said.

He didn't wait for her to answer. He let go of her waist to put his whole arm around her, holding her so that her back was against his chest. He raised his other arm in front of her and used it to firmly clear the way as he herded her toward the closest door, an emergency door with an alarm on it. She knew it would open onto an outdoor courtyard full of picnic tables that would be empty in January. The door was usually propped wide open with a cinder block on summer nights.

Tonight, in the dark, people were heading for the main exit, so she and Graham were like salmon going against the flow as they headed to the much closer emergency exit. The band stopped playing, one guitar after the other petering out mid-chord. More women started screaming, which only added to the chaos.

Emily ducked instinctively as a bottle flew over their heads. She kept moving, the wall of warm man protecting her, his body all around her. The crowd jostled them—well, it jostled him. She only felt everything secondhand, a vibration at her back as his body absorbed any impact. In an amazingly short time, a matter of seconds, Emily and her bodyguard pushed open the silver bar of the emergency exit and burst into the crisp, cold air of the empty courtyard.

"Go on." He let go of her so suddenly that she took a couple more steps before it registered that he'd changed directions and gone back to catch the door before it shut. No alarm was sounding; it had probably never been armed after the summer. Graham reached in, leaning in with his shoulder, and handed out another woman. Another. Then a steady stream of men and women started pouring out of the open door, dozens of people filling up the patio, bringing their loud and excited chatter out into the cold January night.

She lost sight of him.

Her ex, Foster Bentson, hustled out the door instead. Foster looked around the growing crowd, but there was no sharpness in his gaze, no efficient scan of the situation. Instead, Foster looked nervous, peeking back over his shoulder as he put distance between himself and the fight inside. Emily watched him for a moment. That wasn't nervousness; it was guilt. He looked like a child afraid someone had seen him filch an extra dessert.

"Em! Hey, Em!" One of Foster's friends, Doug, called to her from the rapidly growing outdoor crowd. "Have you seen Foster and Mike?"

She pointed briefly. "Foster's over there."

Tarzan had disappeared back into the jungle silently. Emily couldn't do anything about it except wait and hope she'd see him again. Being Jane had its sucky side.

Emily crossed her arms to keep herself warm. It wasn't freezing, but it was still in the forties, typical January weather around here. It was cold enough that she hoped the crowd would be able to go back inside shortly. She'd dressed for her night out in something fun and feminine, not warm. Her legs were bare from mid-thigh to the tops of her cowboy boots. She was going to get real cold, real quick.

Instead of walking over to Foster, Doug hollered at his friend to come over to them. The guys greeted each other like they hadn't seen each other in months instead of minutes, performing some kind of an arm wrestler's grip of a handshake and a bump of shoulders.

Oh, yeah. You're a couple of he-men, the pair of you.

Emily looked around the growing crowd, but Graham was gone. It had been nice of him to get her out of the bar, but considering the way he'd helped the next few women as well, he'd just been a gentleman. He hadn't wanted to have a drink with her, and he didn't want to stick around and talk to her now. She wasn't his Jane.

"Mike's still inside," Foster said. "I don't know what

happened. Some guy just pushed him, and next thing I knew, pool cues were flying."

And then you ran outside to be safe and left Mike to fend for himself in there?

No wonder Foster had come out looking so guilty. He and Doug stared at one another in silence for a moment.

"But Mike can hold his own," Doug offered.

"Oh, yeah. Mike can handle it." Foster sounded eager to believe it.

"Yeah. Mike's fine."

Emily rolled her eyes even as she kept her arms crossed against the cold. "Whether Mike can handle himself or not, I'm sure he'd appreciate some backup." She was half-tempted to go back inside, just to demonstrate how a loyal friend should act. But Mike was Foster's friend, not hers.

Foster looked irritated. "Mike's fine."

"And you're a wimp." Then she smiled at him, very sweetly, just as he'd been begging her to do all night.

Foster opened his mouth, looking offended as all get-out, ready to tell her off.

Bring it, wimp. She was *so* in a mood for a fight. Nothing was going her way tonight. She'd come here to blow off some steam with girlfriends, because her family had spent the entire Christmas break trying to talk her out of the one career—the one life—she wanted. Talk had turned to ultimatums she couldn't disobey. But her friends hadn't shown up. Her ex had. Then a stranger named Graham had rocked her world just by standing still, but the man couldn't be less interested in her. Frustration of every kind was boiling over.

Foster abruptly shut his mouth and settled for a sneer before he shuffled away a couple of feet.

Awareness prickled down her spine, and she turned around to find Graham back in his silent bodyguard mode, standing just behind her. He was scanning the crowd again, but he spared her a glance as she looked at him. He nodded.

Great. Apparently he communicated in nods, which she'd already misinterpreted once. She kept her arms crossed and crossed her ankles, too, squeezing her thighs together to keep warm, and tried communicating with words. "That was my ex and his friend."

"I figured that out."

Ah, he speaks. Emily waited, but that was apparently all Graham was inclined to say.

She tried again. "He's harmless, but it was nice of you to step in earlier by the bathrooms. You don't have to keep being my bodyguard, though. I can handle him."

"There's no gate in this fence," he said. "We're penned in if the fight spills outdoors."

Okay, then. He was still in bodyguard mode. She might not need a bodyguard, but he'd be a heck of a good one, always on duty, always making people think twice with that air of danger about him.

She rubbed her arms. "The only way in and out is the front door where they check the IDs. We won't be leaving for a while."

"If the fight comes out here, we'll have to go over the fence. I'll give you a hand." He glanced at her, and she knew, without a doubt, he was judging how much she weighed and how easy or difficult it would be to toss her over. It was a purely practical evaluation. There was nothing sexual in that look.

He nodded toward one section of the fence. "We'll go there. I can see between the planks that there are no shrubs on the other side to get tangled in."

It wasn't that he was dangerous, she realized. It was that he was prepared to handle danger. "Do you always have an exit plan?"

"Always."

She'd benefited from his last exit plan when they'd been inside, but it was kind of sad that he'd had one when he could have been smiling at her and enjoying a beer instead. Expecting the worst at all times must wear a person out.

"This bar usually isn't this bad. Just a fistfight that's over before it's started, maybe one a week. This one's probably over already. You won't have to throw me over any fences." She patted his arm without thinking, a couple of firm slaps. It was the same way she'd pat her horse's neck after they'd worked the cattle.

Atta boy. We're done now; you don't have to keep watching the herd.

But this was no beast under her hand. This was a man, with hard muscles and an even harder expression on his face.

She pulled her hand back, embarrassed at her impulse, and tucked her hands back under her arms. She uncrossed her ankles, then crossed them the other way, trying to stay warm. There was just enough of a breeze to make the ruffles on her dress lift and ripple.

Graham didn't look cold. In fact, he looked pretty comfortable outside. It was as if now that he'd assessed the situation and located his alternate exit, he was content to wait it out.

Emily wished everyone were that way. The drama gearing up around them was ridiculous. While the men all puffed out their chests and claimed they could have done something if they'd needed to, a group of girls hung all over each other, sobbing, not two feet away. Emily found their drama even worse than the men's bragging. She just couldn't summon up any sympathy for perfectly healthy, perfectly capable women who acted like they were dying.

"Did you see how close they got to me? I swear to *God*, I thought I was going to die."

Emily glanced at Graham. He'd crossed his arms against the cold, too, but he was watching her instead of the crowd, for once. Great. She'd probably been rolling her eyes or wrinkling her nose in disapproval. Her family teased her about the faces she made all the time, so it was entirely possible that she hadn't been keeping her thoughts to herself.

She could pretend she wasn't embarrassed, but it was harder to pretend she wasn't cold. The breeze was pretty brisk, but surely the police were on their way. It took a little while for them to get this far out of town, but they'd be here soon to sort out the action inside. Maybe the patio crowd would be stuck out here for another half an hour, tops. She'd survive.

The cluster of girls weren't cold. They had each other to hug and weep upon, of course, but some had a different strategy. One woman chose a man from the crowd and zeroed in on him, tiptoeing over to him in little baby steps. She clasped her hands and blew on them like they were already frozen solid. "I'm so sorry to bother you, but could I borrow just the edge of your coat? Just to tuck my hands under the hem for a minute? It's so freezing out here." Within a matter of seconds, she had the man eating out of her cold hands, taking off his coat and laying it over her shoulders while she thanked him as if he'd done something extraordinary—as if she hadn't maneuvered him into doing just that.

Emily knew how to play that game, just as she knew how to flash some cleavage to catch a bartender's attention. She simply didn't want to. It took too much energy to keep up the golly-gee-whiz facade. It felt a little demeaning to her, to have to act like an innocent child in order to be thought of as cute. She hadn't been able to sustain it very long with Foster, and Foster hadn't liked her much when she'd acted more like herself and less like a helpless doll.

Still, the girl in the borrowed coat was undoubtedly warmer than Emily at the moment. Girls who acted cute got all the attention.

Not from Graham.

Emily had given him a hearty handshake instead of a cute tilt of her head, and yet, for whatever reason, Graham had gotten her to safety first before helping anyone else.

No wonder Graham was so darned appealing. She hadn't asked him to step in when Foster was harassing her; he just had. She hadn't felt helpless when the fight had broken out, but he'd protected her, anyway. He had to be interested in her, didn't he?

Graham walked a few steps to stand on the other side of her, just close enough to be in her personal space.

"Here, try turning this way," he said. With one hand on her arm, he angled her so that she was once more standing with her back to his chest, but they weren't touching this time. The ruffles of her dress fell still.

"What—what are you doing?" she asked.

"It feels less cold if the wind's at your back."

But of course, he'd blocked the wind for her with his larger body without her having to pout or flirt or even flatly ask him to.

If the man was trying to seduce her without touching her, he was succeeding. Now that Emily thought about it, the literary Jane wasn't a cute or adorable character. She never manipulated anyone. She'd just been herself, lost in a jungle, and a man had swooped in to save her because he'd wanted to, not because she'd flirted with him first.

She looked at Graham over her shoulder. "Now the wind's not at my back. It's at yours."

"That was the idea." The ghost of a smile touched his lips. He looked so unconcerned, standing behind her, but he had to be cold. It was forty-something degrees out, and he was human.

"You'll freeze to death," she said.

"That's doubtful."

She did roll her eyes then.

He shrugged, a small movement of his shoulder. "It's not that windy. More of a brisk breeze."

"It's still cold, no matter how much wind there is or isn't." She hesitated, all her thoughts about not being fake or manipulative swirling in her head. She hoped she wouldn't come across that way. "I know we don't know each other, but if you put your arm around me again, it would keep us both warmer."

He didn't move for the longest moment.

She hadn't played the game right. She should've smiled when she'd said that and tilted her head just so, maybe run a finger over his arm. Or she could've just said she needed to warm up and then leaned into him with a giggle and puppy dog eyes.

Too late now. She'd been straightforward, and it would be too psycho if she suddenly switched gears. So she shrugged her own shrug, as casual as his had been. "I'd feel a little less guilty if I was helping to keep you warm, too. That's all." Pretending her pride wasn't stung, she crossed her ankles the other way and studied the pattern of swirls that had been tooled into the pointed toes of her leather boots.

His arms came around her so gently, the only thing startling was how very warm he felt. He stepped closer, so his chest touched her back. His square-toed boots mingled with her fancy ones.

"Nothing to feel guilty about," he said. "There was no

sense in both of us getting windblown, so I thought I'd stand on this side."

"But this is even warmer, for both of us."

"I can't argue with that."

His voice was close to her ear. No, not his voice—his lips. His mouth. She hadn't meant to use near-freezing temperatures to indulge in a little fantasy with this man, but being wrapped in his arms was delicious.

"For the record, I wouldn't normally put my hands on a woman in the first half hour that I've met her," he said. "My mother would call it 'getting handsy.'"

He had a deep voice. She shivered, and pretended it was from the cold. "It's forty degrees out. Believe me, all I'm thinking is that you're warm, not handsy."

He chuckled, which surprised her, because his expression hadn't been anything but grave from the hallway to the bar to the patio. "My mother drilled it into my head that girls don't like guys who get handsy. I should have dated more in the winter."

"Look how we're standing. We look like a prom photo. You're not being any more handsy than a boy who gets to put his arms around his prom date for the camera while his teachers are chaperoning. Pretty innocent stuff."

"I don't know about innocent intentions at prom," he murmured from his prom position behind her. "I think I was a pretty handsy date. Yours wasn't?"

"I'd had my hair done at a salon. I didn't want him to mess it up." She loved this, being able to just turn her head a little to the side to have a private conversation with Graham, cheek to cheek. "I think I scared him off early in the evening when he went in for a kiss. I said, 'Don't touch my hair.' Maybe it was more like a shriek. *Don't touch my hair.* He barely touched any part of me after that, not even for the slow dances."

She felt Graham's smile even before she peeked at him out of the corner of her eye. He held her just right, his arms loosely crossed over hers, hands resting at her waist, no awkwardness in trying to avoid touching certain parts of her, no accidentally-on-purpose brush against her breasts, either. It was heaven to be with a man who knew what he was doing.

"Whoever your date was, he's kicking himself every time he remembers his prom," Graham said. "An opportunity to hold a pretty girl doesn't come along every day. Fortune favors the brave."

"And you are the brave?"

He paused a fraction of a second. "Back then."

"What about now?"

"I got older. I'm a very, very good boy now." He murmured those words close to her ear, this man who knew what he was doing. Her breath left her in a rush of want, her body reacting instantly with a heavy ache deep inside. *A very, very good boy...*

She turned her head to see more of his profile. He had hard features, nothing of the prettiness of the theater majors at her college, none of the country club grooming of the aspiring business majors. Graham was still keeping an eye on the crowd around them, the way he narrowed his eyes causing little lines to fan at their corners. She felt that same thrill of being protected; she felt that same tug of sympathy for a man who never dropped his guard.

"At least now you won't freeze to death for my sake," she said. "You already took a few punches for me tonight. I'm sorry about that."

"I did?"

"On the way out of the bar."

"Nothing to be sorry for. That was just some pushing and shoving. No one landed a decent hit."

And it wouldn't have fazed you if they had.

He was older, stronger, tougher than the other guys. Stronger than she was, although she thought of herself as both strong and strong-willed—stubborn, her mother called it—and she needed to continue being both if she ever hoped to live the life she wanted. But always being strong could wear a person out.

So tonight…

Why couldn't she be Jane for just one night? Not the strongest, not in charge, not the decision maker. What could be the harm in spending a little time with a man who knew what he was doing?

Chapter Three

Graham had no idea what he was doing.

His plan had been set: he was checking out of the world, going to live in isolation on a cattle ranch, which sounded like going to live in Siberia. Good. He was battered and tired and ready to retreat from the human race. He'd be done with society and all the empty social niceties, officially, tomorrow.

And yet here he was, standing in the crisp, clean air with his arms around a woman who was warm and beautiful, young and full of the future. What the hell was he doing?

Starting tomorrow morning at sunrise, he'd report for duty, so to speak, at the James Hill Ranch. His uncle Gus was the foreman there, and had been for a long time. Word must have traveled through the family that Graham had left the Marine Corps, then left the corporate business world, and now left grad school. For thirty years, Uncle Gus had been a benignly neglectful bachelor uncle, but he must have decided it was time to pay attention to his nephew. The offer had come out of the blue.

Graham didn't know anything about horses. The closest he ever got to cattle was seeing them out the car window as he drove the highways between military bases. That meant he was coming to his new job with no skills, so he'd only be good for the grunt work. He was going to get worked as hard as he'd ever worked in the Marine Corps, digging ditches and hauling sandbags like the lowest-ranking new recruit.

It had been a long time since he'd been the low man on the totem pole. Graham had left the service at the rank of captain. He'd been a company commander, personally responsible for the training and well-being of two hundred Marines, charged with leading them on every assigned mission, anywhere in the world they were sent.

No longer—and that was fine. Graham looked forward to the oblivion that hard labor would grant him. He'd be responsible for no one and nothing. He'd be bone tired every night; he'd sleep. He'd wake up the next day and do it all over again. He expected nothing more out of life.

So why was he standing here with one light and lovely Emily Davis in his arms?

Some of the crowd had started to go back inside. Graham watched as they hustled right back out again. The sound of men shouting and bottles shattering mixed with the hyped-up chatter of the outdoor crowd.

"It sounds like a war zone in there," Emily said.

Not quite. But Graham had no desire to start dredging up memories from Afghanistan, so he said nothing.

"The poor Keller family. They bought this place just a few years ago. I went to high school with their son, Jason. Sounds like they aren't going to have much furniture left."

"So you're a local?"

He could have bitten his tongue out. What was he doing? Making small talk? Trying to get to know her?

"Sometimes," she said. "I was born in San Antonio, but I've got family around here. I grew up going between San Antonio and Austin, Austin to San Antonio. I never went beyond that little hundred-mile stretch until I started college in Oklahoma."

He said nothing.

"I'm nearly done there. Nearly. Not soon enough."

He closed his eyes for a moment. A college girl with her life ahead of her. His was so empty in comparison. He shouldn't have his hands on her, not even in an innocent prom pose.

"How about you?" she asked quietly, and he could tell she'd turned her head to look at him.

He opened his eyes. "Just passing through."

Glass shattered inside the bar.

"We may be here awhile." She sighed and relaxed into Graham's arms just as easily as if they were old friends who hung out together all the time. "Every time it sounds like it's quieting down, it spins right back up again."

The blue ruffles at her waist tickled the inside of his wrist.

Old friends. Sure.

The last time he'd held a woman in his arms for any length of time, he'd been in bed and they'd just shared some very satisfying sex. He didn't mind falling asleep like this with a woman, spooning when they were still appreciative of each other's bodies. He couldn't remember the specific woman and the specific bed of the last time, though. Not at the moment, not with his arms full of Emily. It had been a long while, he knew that much.

He'd gone long stretches before, of course, due to deployments: a year in the Middle East, half a year on an aircraft carrier. He was a civilian now, no geography forcing him into celibacy, yet he'd had no interest in any of his fellow grad students while pushing through this past semester. Working for his uncle on a ranch far from civilization wasn't going to require much of a sacrifice when it came to his social life. He didn't have one, and he hadn't cared.

Until now. The night before he was about to bury himself in the middle of nowhere, he was holding a woman who was making him remember things that were worth living for.

Maybe this was like quitting smoking. One planned for it, wanting it and dreading it at the same time, until finally, the night before officially quitting, one last cigarette, better than all the ones that had come before, was savored.

Emily Davis was his last cigarette.

He wasn't going to sleep with her. Even if she'd have him, he would be all wrong for her. He wanted to make sure she got out of this bar safely and back to her bright life, and then he'd drive west two more counties and find the ranch where his uncle worked.

But in the meantime, whether he had minutes with her or hours, he'd savor this woman who was buoyant and charming—and unafraid to tell a man to go to hell—before he began his self-imposed exile.

There couldn't be any harm in that.

Emily felt something change in the way Graham was holding her. It wasn't a big difference, just an ease in his shoulders. His hand relaxed, fingers resting on her hip.

She could stay like this forever, but he'd said he was just passing through. The disappointment almost hurt.

You're leaving for college in three days. Did you expect him to be waiting here for you when you came back on spring break?

She sighed, which only made her sink more cozily into his arms. How terrible, to be so fascinated by a man whom she might never see again.

Might never see again. It depended where he was going. It depended where he'd come from.

"You're just passing through on your way to where?" she asked.

The roaring of motorcycle engines made an answer impossible. Five motorcycles or maybe more pulled in, from what Emily could see through the thin gaps between the wood planks of the fencing. The moment they killed their engines, the patio conversations resumed.

Not hers. She felt the tension return to Graham's body. He let go of her, keeping only one hand on her waist, the position he'd taken just before they'd run from the bar fight.

"We should go," he said.

"Bikers stop here all the time. They like to ride out here because there's no traffic. It's scenic in the daytime." She hated to see him this tense again. She smiled, but she refrained from giving him another reassuring horse slap. "They aren't as scary as they look. They're just hanging out with their clubs. They're sure going to be surprised when they open that door and walk in to that fight."

Graham didn't smile with her. "They're not out for a Sunday ride. There's a difference between a club and a gang. Whichever these men are, there are at least two different groups here tonight. Two different jackets."

She looked around the patio crowd. Even Jason had come outside, abandoning his bar after calling the police, no doubt. None of the bikers had come outside. "You think this is a fight between gangs?"

"It's no coincidence more bikers just showed up. This is going to get worse before it gets better."

Graham had that aura of readiness about him again, the one that said danger was coming. He'd been right last time. She wasn't inclined to question him now. "Okay, then. Let's go."

"Is there anyone you came with that we need to get out?" Graham asked.

Just as she said no, there was another commotion at the doorway. Mike came barreling toward them, crashing into Foster, pushing him another foot closer to Emily.

"Where were you? Where the hell were you, Foster? Doug?" Mike was spitting out their names. His lip was bleeding. His eye was swelling shut. "You gotta get me out of here, now. They're pulling out brass knuckles and chains. Knives, man, knives."

"Is he a friend of yours?" Graham's voice was back at her ear, level and patient, but his stance was ready to move, chomping at the bit to head for the fence.

"Not really. We go to the same college." But Mike looked like hell, and she felt sorry for him, so she stepped just far enough away from Graham to tap Mike on the shoulder. "Hey. We're leaving. Follow us."

Then Graham's hand was at the small of her back as they walked directly toward the section of the fence he'd already chosen. He escorted her as courteously as if she'd been dressed in high heels instead of cowboy boots. But since she was in boots, she made a little run at the fence when they were still a few feet away, wanting a bit of speed so she'd have the momentum to run halfway up and reach the top with two hands. To pull herself over, she had to walk herself up the planking, hoping for some traction between the leather of her soles and the grain of the wood. She felt one strong, warm hand on her backside, giving her that extra lift that made it easier to haul herself up and over. She dropped onto the dirt of the parking lot on the other side of the fence.

She tugged her dress back in place. More hands grabbed the top of the fence. Mike's battered face appeared at the top, but he, too, was struggling to get over. One second later, he got almost too much of a boost to handle. He landed next to her, barely keeping on his feet. Foster came over next, same way. Doug.

The police arrived, red and blue lights shining on the planks of the fence as sirens screamed through the parking lot, passing them on their way around the building to the front of the bar. Emily shielded her eyes from the flashing and looked up to the top of the fence. When it was dark once more, Graham came sailing over the top, just one hand on the fence, clearing it cleanly, as if he'd flipped himself up and over a ten-foot fence a hundred times before.

You, Tarzan. For sure.

Mike grabbed Foster's sleeve. "Come on, let's go. I can't get a police record. You know what my father would do." Doug and Foster took off toward the parking lot with him, but Mike suddenly changed direction and stuck his hand out to Graham for a quick shake. "Thanks, man."

Then Emily was alone with Graham in the dark. The planking of the fence was all that stood between her and the sounds of turmoil and outright violence on the other side. She stood next to Graham and felt safe.

"Where's your car parked?" he asked.

Her heart fell a little. She didn't want him to pack her off in her car, but what was the alternative while the police raided the bar? To hide here in the shadows of the red and blue lights and continue their little get-to-know-you chat?

"I'm parked around front."

More motorcycles entered the parking lot. Another sheriff's car pulled in right behind.

Graham's hand on her waist came as no surprise. "Mine's back here. I'll drive you around the front."

Ask me to go somewhere else with you to get a drink.

But he didn't. His car was actually an SUV, new and expensive, an exotic European brand. He shadowed her all the way to the passenger door, shutting her into the leather-upholstered luxury before jogging around the front of the vehicle to reach his own door.

The upscale SUV meant two things to Emily. First, Graham had money, which she should have guessed. He was a man who knew what he was doing and how to handle the world around him. It made sense that he'd be on top of his financial world, too. Second, the sexiest man in her world really was just passing through. No one drove a vehicle like this in ranch country. She sat in her bucket seat, feeling a million miles away from him on the other side of the extra-wide console.

He started the engine. "What kind of car am I looking for?"

Ask me to go out for a bite to eat.

"I drive a pickup truck." Not the most feminine thing to drive, but she did live in ranch country—or she would, when she finished her degree and her mother had no more leverage to wield over her choices.

Graham's hands looked strong on the smooth leather of the steering wheel as he casually backed out of the parking spot. Emily would have hated to get a scratch on the paint, but he seemed completely oblivious to the fact that his vehicle cost as much as some people's houses.

"That doesn't narrow it down much," he said. "Three quarters of this parking lot are pickup trucks."

"Mine's red," she said.

*With a hitch to tow a horse trailer, because, unlike you,
I am from around here.*

She told him the make and model, an entry-level truck.
She'd bought it from her brother-in-law, a bargain with only
seventy thousand well-cared-for miles on it. She'd added
another ten thousand miles, driving it to Oklahoma and
back at the start and end of every semester, and from her
mother's house to her uncle's ranch every chance she got—
like this weekend. She'd come to spend her last weekend of
the winter break back at her uncle's ranch. She'd be muck-
ing out stalls tomorrow morning. Voluntarily.

Emily flicked one of her ruffles into place. Yeah, her
girly evening was rapidly coming to a close. Being taken
care of by a man who was tough and strong had been sexy.
Being taken care of by a man who was tough and strong
and rich should have been even better, but instead, it only
drove home that this was a fantasy with no hope of becoming anything else. He wasn't from around here. He wasn't
staying around here, and he wanted to drop her off so he
could get on his way.

At Graham's soft curse, she looked up from her ruffles.
The entire front parking lot was flooded by police cars
and motorcycles. Her poor truck was one of an entire row
stuck behind a fleet of sheriffs' vehicles. Graham stopped
the SUV. She wouldn't be going anywhere for a while.

She glanced at Graham. His eyes were closed. He
rubbed his forehead with the fingers of one hand, disgust
written all over his face.

Her heart had already been sinking. Now it hit bottom.
The man did not want to be stuck with her all night long.
It hurt, because she would have loved to spend more time
with him.

Her pride rose to deal with the pain. He didn't want to

be stuck with her? Luckily for him, he wasn't. She wasn't helpless.

Say good-night, Jane.

"Well, thank you again for helping me get out of the bar. And for helping me get over the fence. Helping *all* of us get over the fence." As long as she was relying on her own pride, she wanted to point out that the guys had needed boosts, too.

"I'm sorry," he said. "Really sorry. I wasn't thinking—"

"Nothing to be sorry for," she said, imitating his earlier words. She didn't want to hear the man apologize for not wanting her company. She slipped her fingertips into the top of her left boot and under the edge of her calf-high sock, where she'd stashed the key to her truck. "You travel safely to wherever you're going. I'm… I'm glad I got to meet you. Thanks again." She opened the door.

"What are you doing?"

"Good night, Graham."

"You can't leave."

As if she'd stay now, when he'd wanted nothing more than to put her in her truck so that he could get on to wherever he was going. She slipped off the high seat to land on the ground outside, nice and solid on her own two feet, her smile plastered in place as if her disappointment wasn't choking her. As she closed her door, she caught a glimpse as Graham threw his gear shift into park and opened his door. He was fast; she'd taken only a step in the direction of her red truck before he rounded the hood of the SUV.

"Get back in the truck."

She almost, *almost* obeyed that tone of voice, reaching for the door handle before she snatched her hand back. "Did you just give me an order?"

"You can't stand out here." He wasn't looking at her, but over her, that sharp gaze on the police scene behind her.

"I'm not going to stand anywhere. I'll sit in my truck until the police leave. My phone's in there. My jacket's in there. I won't freeze."

"It isn't safe."

"I'll be just fine as can be. No one is going to bother me with this many cops around."

He yanked the door open. "Your truck isn't bulletproof. Let's go."

"Bulletproof?"

Wow, the poor man really was too much on alert—but then Emily heard the hoarse voice of a cop from behind her, sounding like something from a movie: "Let me see your hands!"

She whipped around to see cops running from the bar back to their cruisers, opening their doors and crouching behind them as they drew their guns.

"Put your gun on the ground!" ordered the hoarse cop, who was still standing, his weapon drawn and aimed at the front door of the bar.

Two hands on her waist yanked her back toward the SUV. Graham practically tossed her into the cab headfirst, then she felt his hand squarely on her rear end, shoving her farther into the cab. "Go. Get behind the wheel."

She scrambled over the center console as Graham crowded her, climbing in behind her. She was still twisting around to get her butt in the seat when he slammed the gear shift down to the number one and pointed toward the field beyond the parking lot. "That way."

The SUV started rolling forward in first gear. The driver's seat was set for him, too far back for her to reach the pedals well, so she had to sit on the edge and hang on to the steering wheel to reach the brake. In the passenger seat, Graham ducked his chin to look into the side view mirror, then he turned around to look through the center seats and out the back window.

She'd just gotten her foot on the brake when she heard the unmistakable sound of a police megaphone. "Come out with your hands up."

"Jeez," she said, and switched to the gas pedal, steering with one hand as she used her other to feel around for the seat controls. The only way out of the parking lot, thanks to the patrol car barricade, was to drive cross-country through the scrub brush. "Your paint job is going to take a beating."

"It'll be just fine as can be."

Wait—that was something she'd said. Was he being a smart aleck? She didn't have time to decide; she was adjusting the driver's seat with one hand as she steered toward the edge of the parking lot with the other, all while glancing from the view out the windshield down to the unusual drivetrain indicator. "How do you put it in four-wheel drive?"

"You don't need to. It'll adjust to the terrain."

"Okay. Hang on."

He braced one hand against the roof as they left the parking lot for the fields. They were bounced out of their seats a time or two, but she could feel the vehicle's drivetrain adjusting, each wheel gripping individually when it got traction as she drove over hardened grooves in the earth, the muddy remains of a creek bed and the sandy soil beyond. She slowed once they'd gone the distance of a football field or so, but Graham gestured for her to keep moving while he kept watch out the back window.

"Take us all the way out to the highway."

She hesitated.

"Bullets fly more than a hundred yards," he said.

"If I remember rightly, we're going toward a creek that probably isn't dry."

"It'll wash the dirt off the paint job."

Definitely a smart aleck.

"You might want to fasten your seat belt, then." She let the SUV roll forward as she pulled her seat belt across her chest and buckled it. "You're going to find out how good your suspension is the hard way."

He looked at her instead of the parking lot scene for a moment, one of his infrequent smiles touching one corner of his mouth. "She's more than a pretty paint job. She was built for this."

"So I've heard." The manufacturer was legendary for getting its start building safari vehicles. Emily put her boot on the gas again, pushing their speed a little more. "If I didn't feel like I was running for my life, I'd be enjoying this."

Graham turned around to face front and pulled his seat belt across his chest, too, as she drove on in silence. She couldn't say he relaxed, but he wasn't keeping a constant lookout behind them any longer. That had to be a good sign. Her knowledge of bullets was limited to her uncle's rifles on the ranch. She didn't know how far a police handgun could fire—and no one knew if the fighters in the club were armed, or with what. But if Graham was less concerned now, then so was she.

Foolish little Jane, putting all your trust in this man who just swooped in out of nowhere.

But gosh, he'd done just that. She was so very aware of him, of the size of him, the energy of his body in the close interior. Aware of the smell of his warm skin dominating the vehicle's cool leather. Of the strength in his arm braced against the ceiling, the same arm he'd braced against the iron-edged bar to protect her when the only thing they'd known about each other had been their names.

She knew more about him now: how he reacted in an emergency, how he helped strangers without a second thought. How he'd tried not to be too *handsy* at a school dance, once upon a time, because he'd listened to his mama's advice, like a young man should.

She liked everything she knew—except for one thing. He was only with her because the police had given him no choice.

If it weren't for that, she'd really be enjoying this.

Chapter Four

The creek was low at this time of year, so Emily drove
Graham's SUV through it easily enough. From there, it was
just a short distance to the paved road, a two-lane highway
that ran from the outskirts of Austin through hundreds of
miles of cattle country. Emily headed west, away from
the bar, away from Austin. There were no streetlights to
cut through the black night, so the lights of another emergency vehicle were bright in the rearview mirror, although
the red and blue flashes were at least a mile behind them.
She watched in the mirror as the lights dipped below the
horizon, adding to the distant glow of the police cars sur-
rounding the bar.

She whistled low. "Police are still showing up. Do you
think there was a shootout? Could you see what was—"

"No."

His answer stopped her short. There was an awkward
moment of silence while she wondered why he was so curt.

"We would have heard it if shots were fired," he said.

"That's good. I hate to think of anyone in uniform getting shot in the line of duty."

Graham was silent.

Emily didn't mind. "This is a Thursday night that'll be talked about for a while around here. I've never seen that many patrol cars out here. We're not usually this violent out in the country."

"I can believe that. It's empty out here. It's as dark as…"

She stole a peek at him when his sentence trailed off into nothing. There was no trace of a sexy smile, no smart-aleck grin, either. He was in perfect profile, the lines of his forehead, nose, jaw all highlighted by the glow of the dashboard lights. He might as well have been carved from marble for all the expression his face didn't show.

"As dark as what?" she asked.

"As anywhere I've ever been," he finished flatly.

Emily looked out the windshield at the passing white dashes of the endless center line. She supposed being expressionless wasn't the worst thing he could be. He could look impatient or irritated with the fact that he was stuck with her when he'd been ready to drop her at her truck and leave. Instead, he just looked stoic. Stoically surviving this additional time with her.

She felt just as bad as she had in the parking lot. She'd tried to leave him when he'd started saying *I'm sorry*. It wasn't her fault he'd thrown her into his SUV when the cops had started ducking for cover.

She slowed the SUV and made a U-turn in the middle of the empty road. Once they were facing the direction of the bar, she pulled a good car's length off the road and put the vehicle into park. She left the lights on, so other cars would see them on the shoulder, if another car was actually on this rural road. He didn't ask her what she was doing.

She explained, anyway. "We can see the glow of the sheriff's lights from behind that little rise in the road. When the red and blue cut off, we'll know the coast is clear."

And you can take me back to my pickup and get rid of me at the first possible moment.

"All right." He opened his glove box and took out a cell phone, checked the screen, then tossed it to the center console.

Of course. He probably had someone to check in with, someone from the place he'd just left or the place he was going to. He couldn't make a call with her sitting right here, staring at him and listening to every word. She'd never felt like such a burden before.

She hated it. She pretended she didn't and let go of the steering wheel. "You've got a real nice ride here. It was fun to drive, considering the circumstances. But, you know, that whole little episode was pretty intense. Think I'll walk it off a bit while we wait."

"Emily."

Jeez, he said her name like her mother would, *Emily* said in a tone that meant *be sensible*.

"No bullet is going to come over that rise and get me." She unfastened her seat belt.

"You'll freeze."

"No, I won't. I'm just going to stretch my legs." She opened the door.

"Emily—"

She dropped down the foot to the gravel shoulder of the road and shut her door. The emergency lights flashed on the horizon. The air temperature hadn't fallen any further. This was as cold as it was going to get tonight. Not too bad—if she'd had her jacket. She started walking and swung her arms, too. It did feel good to shake off some of the tension.

She avoided the bright headlights and walked around the back of the vehicle to the other side. Graham's door opened and the interior lights came on, highlighting the rounded bulk of his shoulder muscles under that navy shirt. He stepped out and slammed the door shut. In the sudden shadows, he handed her a coat.

Oh, Tarzan. He was still taking care of her when he'd rather be free of her.

"Thanks. You didn't have to do that." She held the coat in one hand.

He leaned his back against the door and crossed his ankles, apparently prepared to relax out in the cold air. "You might as well put it on, if you're going to walk around while we wait."

"But now you'll be the one freezing without it." Although the headlights were pointed away from them, they still illuminated her little piece of the night enough that she could see her breath as a mist in the cold.

He shrugged in the shadows. "I'll get back in the SUV if I can't take it. If you feel the need to walk, you wear it."

She swirled his coat around her shoulders like a cape, feeling a little bit sheepish. She didn't want to admit that she didn't need to walk anywhere, for any reason. "I thought—I thought you might want some privacy to make a call."

"There's no cell reception out here."

"Oh. Right." That must have been why he'd tossed his cell phone, not because he couldn't make a call in her presence. To walk or not walk—which would make her look less dumb?

He tucked his hands into his front pockets. "Are you scared of me?"

With his face in shadows, she paid more attention to his tone of voice. He sounded concerned, actually concerned about her, Emily, the girl that the boys didn't always like because they couldn't beat her in a roping contest. A man who was concerned about her—it tugged at her heart. It made her weak in the knees. She was scared by how hard she wanted something she hadn't thought she needed in her life. She *didn't* need it; she just liked it. Loved it.

"When the police drew their weapons, I pushed you into my SUV pretty abruptly," he said. "Maybe I scared you. I didn't mean to. If the police needed to take cover, then we did, too."

"I'm not scared of you." That was sort of a lie, but she wasn't scared of him the way he meant. She kept her chin up and pretended her heart wasn't pounding just because he was talking to her with concern in his voice.

"I can imagine a woman might feel uneasy being out in the middle of nowhere with a stranger. I promise you, you're safe."

His hands were still tucked in his front pockets as he leaned against the door. He was being as physically non-threatening as he could be, she realized, putting himself in her shoes and trying to imagine what she might be afraid of. Just—*jeez*. What a good man. Who knew a man like that could swoop in to her local bar from out of nowhere?

He was watching her. "I'd never push anything farther than a woman wanted to take it."

"Even though you were a handsy prom date?"

A beat of silence. "Even then, I could take no for an answer."

"Because your mama taught you better."

"Some things you don't have to be taught. Of course I wouldn't hurt a woman I wanted to…touch." The slightest smile softened his features, but then he slayed her with a casual wink. "I just can't imagine it would be any fun if *she* wasn't having any fun."

Well.

She couldn't say anything to that. It was amazing she could even stand, because her bones had just turned to mush and she wanted to drop like a ribbon at his feet.

His voice was a gentle rumble in the night. "I'm trying to figure out why you got out of a warm car to stand in the cold air. Twice, not that I'm counting."

"I was trying to give you some space. You didn't plan on being stuck with me all night." Her voice sounded sad. She tried to put a little spunk into it. "In my defense, this wasn't my idea. I can take a hint. I did take the hint, in fact."

"What hint was that?"

"In the parking lot. You were starting the whole 'I'm sorry' speech. 'Sorry, but I've got to get going now. Nice knowin' you.' I understand. You were never obliged to stay with me as long as you did. You could have jumped over that fence anytime you wanted to and left."

His hands stayed in his pockets, but the muscles in his arms were taut, the muscles in his neck showing his tension. He looked away from her. "That wasn't it."

She waited, but he said nothing else. After a moment, she took a step closer to him. "Then what were you saying sorry for?"

He looked back at her with a suddenly fierce expression. "I'm sorry I didn't get you out of there sooner."

"Oh." The look of disgust on his face, she realized, was directed toward himself, not toward her.

"I knew that crowd was going to turn bad. I failed to get you out of there. I was too slow to act on my own intuition, and I put you in danger because of it. Your truck is out of commission now, when it would have been fine if I'd gotten you out of there at the start. You would have been gone before the police arrived. I'm sorry."

"We were only standing at the bar for a minute or two."

"Long enough. I saw the argument starting when we were working our way through the crowd. I should have gotten you out that door instead of following you to the bar in the first place."

Poor Tarzan, always obliged to help the people who wandered into the jungle. She felt a little guilty for soaking up all his protection. She'd done nothing except admire his body, his voice and his profile, while he'd been trying to keep her safe from fists and bullets, literally trying to save her life.

She turned to lean her back against the door, too, shoulder to shoulder with him, so he'd know she wasn't afraid that he was going to physically attack her or anything like that. "It wasn't your job to predict a fight or even to get me out of the bar. It's my turn to apologize. I know I've given you the wrong impression all night, and I'm sorry for that, but I'm not actually the helpless type of female."

"I know that."

"I don't think you do." She glanced up to find him looking down at her.

His gaze dropped to her mouth. "The first words I heard you say were 'go to hell.'"

Her laugh of surprise was a single puff of white that floated away in the night air.

"You damn near made it over that fence before I could get a hand on you to help. This has nothing to do with whether or not I think you're helpless. You're clearly not."

"Then why did you decide to help me?" *Me, out of all the women in that bar?*

She had hopes, high hopes. She wanted to hear him say he'd taken one look at her and felt the same way she had:

here was someone he wanted to get to know better. Someone attractive, appealing—even sexy.

But the moment passed. Then another. He studied the darkness beyond their little pool of light. "You never leave someone behind in battle. Never."

Not sexy. Kind of grim, actually.

"Were you in the military?" she asked.

"Yes. Were you?"

"No." But there was a compliment in there. It wasn't sexy, but it was something. "No one's ever asked me that before. What makes you think I might have served in the military?"

He didn't answer her.

She wanted to see his smile again. She nudged him with her shoulder. "Come on, tell me. Was it my fabulous driving skills? Do you think I'd be good at driving a tank, or what?"

His smile returned briefly. "That wasn't your first time off-roading."

"I couldn't call myself a Texan if I'd never taken a truck off-road."

She wanted to touch him. She'd already stood in the warmth of his arms. Heck, he'd already had his hand on her rear end twice, even if both times had been during an escape.

Fortune favors the brave. Those had been the man's own words.

"You want to know why I thought you might be in the military?" She dared to reach up and touch the back of his neck, the clean skin above his collar. She let her fingers comb through the short hair at the back of his head. "It wasn't this haircut. It's short, but not as short as the soldiers from Fort Hood."

"I'm a civilian now. A regulation haircut would be too...

unnecessary." He didn't shake her off or step away, but he didn't touch her in return, either, except with his gaze.

She let her hand slip over his shoulder lightly before falling away. "I'll tell you what gave it away. It was the way you ordered me to get back in the truck. Do they teach you to bark out orders in that tone of voice? It's scary as hell."

"It didn't work on you." He grumbled those words, which made her smile.

"I'm stubborn like that, and I already know it's not a good trait. I hear about it from my family all the time." She pushed away from the door and turned to face him— which meant she stepped over his crossed ankles with one foot and stood in her mini dress with her legs a little way apart, his boots between hers. The night air was cold on her inner thighs. "But I didn't bark out any orders like a military man, so what made you think I might have served? Come on, talk to me." She gestured toward the red and blue glow on the horizon. "We can't go anywhere, anyway. Was it my haircut?"

She was joking, of course, but her laughter faded at the intensity of his gaze. She couldn't look away, not even when he turned his attention from her eyes to her hair, somewhere near her temple. Her ear. Slowly, so slowly, his gaze followed the length of her hair as it lay on her shoulder, as it curved over her breast, as it disappeared in the open edge of his coat, near her hip.

She wanted him. He was leaning against his vehicle, arms crossed, ankles crossed, not moving a muscle, setting her on fire with a look.

"There's nothing military about your hair," he said quietly, and he looked back up to her eyes. "It was your head. You keep a cool head."

"A cool head." She breathed in cold air, willing herself

to say something, to do something, although her thoughts weren't cool at all. "That's it?"

"That's not all that common." He pushed away from the door and stood before her, a little too close, and not nearly close enough. "You also didn't leave your ex and his friends behind, even though they didn't deserve your help."

Kiss me, kiss me.

But the man didn't move an inch closer. "They were lucky. If I hadn't wanted to dance with you so badly, I would have gotten you out of there before trouble started, and they wouldn't have had you around to bail them out."

Wait—*what?* To heck with her ex and the fight. "You wanted to dance with me?"

"The second that band played anything remotely resembling a slow song. I ignored the beginnings of that fight, because I wanted to see if the band would play something we could dance to. It's the only way to touch a woman you barely know without being too..."

"Handsy?" Dear God, she sounded breathless. She was breathless.

"That's the word."

He'd wanted to touch her from the start. This insane chemistry was the same for both of them.

He didn't reach for her now. Why didn't he reach for her?

"So dancing is an acceptable way to touch a woman you just met." She kept her voice low in the dark.

"Right."

"And we decided keeping someone warm when it's cold out is allowed."

"True." He didn't move.

"Graham." Emily put her palm on his chest and tilted her face up to his. "It's cold out."

He touched her, sliding just one warm hand under her

hair to the back of her neck, pulling her just an inch closer. After a breathless pause, he kissed her. In contrast to that strong hand, his lips were shockingly soft against hers for one unbearably perfect moment. She took a breath when he pulled away, her eyes fluttering open to see him looking down at her, and then he kissed her again.

Harder. This time, his arms came around her, gathering her to his chest. She made a little sound, a groan of relief—finally, they were kissing—and buried her fingers in his hair once more. Their mouths opened; they tasted each other, not tentatively but with certainty, as if they knew already that they'd like the taste and the sensation and the intimacy. *Yes?*

Yes—and then he was kissing her deeply, molding her body against his from chest to hips, so she didn't need to hold herself upright. If she went limp like a ribbon, she wouldn't fall. She'd stay right here, secure in Graham's arms.

The kiss ended. He'd ended it, but they still held each other tight, breaths panting into the night like steam.

He held her a little harder, then let her go just far enough that she could look into his face. Dear God, he looked good when he looked kissed.

He spoke quietly, warm words stirring the air near her cheek. "I need to take you home. Now."

Arousal obliterated her thoughts for a hot moment. She'd never gone to bed with a man on a first date—but she'd never been tempted by Graham.

She swallowed and tried to clear her head enough to work out the logistics. "Where's your home? I thought you were just passing through."

"Not my home. Yours. Let me drive you to your place."

Yes. I want him all to myself. I want him in my bed, this

man who knows what he's doing. But where was she going to take him? To her mother's house? To her uncle's ranch?

"I wish you could," she said, and she meant it. "My apartment is at Oklahoma Tech. I'm staying with family for the winter break."

"Oklahoma Tech." He closed his eyes and rested his forehead against hers, and she knew, she just knew, that he was giving up on the possibility of spending time with her. And she knew, she just knew, that would be a mistake.

For both of them.

So she kissed him again, to feel the thrill of a perfect kiss once more, and to make sure he was a little drunk on the taste of her, before she asked him once more:

"Can I buy you a drink?"

Chapter Five

His last cigarette was going to kill him.

She tasted good on his tongue. She soothed a craving in his brain. Emily Davis was so addicting, he dreaded giving her up tonight.

He was going to have to. She was too young; he was too jaded. She needed to go back to college; he needed the oblivion of hard labor. Geography would take them in opposite directions, as it should. It was inevitable. He was a fool to breathe her in just one more time.

He breathed in anyway, savoring the feminine scent of the woman in his passenger seat as he drove. Maybe it was the floral smell of her shampoo as she lifted her hair from under his jacket's collar and let it fall over her shoulder. It couldn't have been the vanilla lip gloss—he'd kissed off the last of that. Whatever it was, he hadn't predicted how intoxicating he'd find it. Tomorrow, when Emily Davis was gone, he hoped he wouldn't miss it too badly.

He glanced at Emily for the tenth time. She was buckled in, but she still gave him the impression that she was sitting on the edge of her seat. She seemed ready to take on life, even when things were turning bad in bars and parking lots.

He was not. Too much had happened in his life. After the grim truth he'd witnessed firsthand overseas—desperate men had the capacity to cut up a man, to kick a woman, to starve a child—he'd thought the brotherhood with his fellow Marines would balance it out. It hadn't, not quite. He'd thought civilian life would be easier, but it hadn't been, and so he knew he was simply used up. Some human beings made it to old age before they'd used up their reserves. Some humans were old at age ten. Benjamin Graham was old at thirty, but he'd taken that risk when he'd joined the military. He was fine with it.

He wasn't fine with dragging a bright and beautiful woman down before her time, though. In every way, he was wrong for her, and he knew it even when he'd given in and kissed her.

He'd tried to stop before things got too hot. *I need to take you home now*, he'd said, for her sake as well as his. Before they did anything they'd regret, it was best to drive her to her house and then get back on the road to start putting miles between them. She surely had family or friends who would drive her to that bar to get her truck tomorrow.

But she'd misunderstood. She'd thought he needed to take her home to make love to her.

She'd agreed.

I wish you could. Since pretty much every cell of his body—except one tiny, rational corner of his brain—had agreed that taking her home to make love was pretty much the best damned idea in the world, he hadn't corrected her mistake.

She thought the only reason they weren't headed to bed was the fact that she was staying with relatives; he wasn't sure she was wrong. It was humbling to find out his resolve could be so easily overpowered by a young woman from Oklahoma Tech University. But since the red and blue police lights were still visible at the horizon, and since he couldn't keep kissing her in the dark, they were driving somewhere to get a drink. Then he'd see her back to her truck safely and be on his way.

He breathed in deeply.

"It'll be up here on the right after we go around this curve," Emily said, looking out the window with the enthusiasm of someone approaching Disney World.

He hit his turn signal out of habit, although there was no one to signal. They were the only vehicle as far as the eye could see. He was already farther from any semblance of a town than he'd been since—since Afghanistan, to be honest, and he still had a long way to go before he reached Uncle Gus's ranch. The map had shown another sixty miles or so, somewhere in another county, but he wasn't certain without being able to get a signal for his cell phone. He'd craved solitude on a ranch, and he was going to get it.

But not yet. Not tonight.

Around the curve, a building lit up the dark. *Schumer's 24/7 Grocery*, the sign said, glowing yellow above a pair of gas pumps. *Closed Christmas.*

"A gas station?" he asked, glancing at Emily. Any excuse to glance at Emily.

"It's the only other place to go without driving all the way back to Austin. Come on. I'll buy you a drink like the real locals do." Her seat belt was off before he'd pulled into the parking spot in front of the convenience store's door. His tires had barely stopped moving when she opened the door and hopped down in a flutter of blue ruffles, the edges of his coat flapping behind as she wore it like a cape. Apparently, this convenience store was a great place to be.

He followed her through the glass double doors. The smell of beef and wood smoke hit him, so unexpected that he almost looked for the barbecue when he should have been scanning the location for trouble. Habits formed in the Middle East died hard; he scanned. Left to right, check the corners, clear the room.

Clear. This place was safe. The only threat was a white-haired man who glowered at them from behind the cash register.

Emily headed straight for the wall of glass-fronted refrigerators. "That brisket smells amazing, Mr. Schumer. Got any left?"

The man made a scoffing sound. "Sure. Ten pounds, at least. Maybe more."

Emily kept heading down the chips aisle toward the cooler, but she turned around and walked backward as she filled Graham in. "That means no, and he's insulted that I asked. He only makes so much brisket every day. Once it's gone, that's it until tomorrow. People around here have been known to race each other to get here for the last pound."

"I can believe it." It smelled damn good; Emily looked damn good. They'd have to come much earlier next time—

Next time.

There'd be no next time. There shouldn't even be a now.

But there was. He watched Emily open a cooler door. Most of her body was engulfed by his coat, but a few rows of blue ruffles peeked out below the bottom edge, looking as erotic as a forbidden glimpse of black lace. She reached for a six-pack from a lower shelf, and the hem of her short dress rode up the backs of her bare thighs as she bent over. She stood up slowly. When she shook that long, loose hair back, he knew she'd been doing it deliberately—and for his pleasure.

To have a woman like Emily doing anything strictly for his pleasure…

She looked over her shoulder at him with a come-and-get-me smile.

He almost did. Every fiber of his being wanted to walk down that aisle and pull her close again. Her body had felt like heaven under his hands on the highway.

He leaned an elbow on the shelf of pretzels and rubbed his forehead, trying to keep his thoughts in the right order. The tasks required were simple. Alpha: see Emily safely back to her own truck. Bravo: say goodbye, firmly and forever. Charlie: get his sorry ass to Uncle Gus's ranch by sunrise.

An alternate plan was vying for precedence in his mind. Alpha: spend the night with Emily, because she wanted to spend the night with him. Bravo:

There was no second task. It all started and ended with Emily. This last cigarette was all-consuming.

Relax, Graham. You'll be able to live without it. You're not addicted to anything.

He sighed and met her by the register.

The owner didn't ring them up. "I need to see some ID."

She's not that young. Please don't be that young.

"Are you serious?" Emily asked. "I graduated from high school with your granddaughter."

"Hmpf."

"You were there."

The man didn't move.

"Nicole and I are the same age. Twenty-two."

Thank God.

"You know that, Mr. Schumer," she said, clearly offended. Maybe she was embarrassed to be carded. Graham could remember hating that, also. He couldn't remember now why he'd been so impatient to be older than twenty-two.

"I need to see some ID." The angry grandpa was just being stubborn now.

"Fine." Emily bent over again, slipping her hand into her boot. That mini dress was short, but not quite short enough. It never rode up to a point that would be indecent, but damn, it got close.

She straightened with a driver's license in her hand, along with a credit card she'd stashed in her boot. He already knew there was nowhere for her to stash it in that dress, thanks to a long and hot kiss on the side of a dark and cold highway.

He looked away from her hemline. Angry Grandpa was glowering at him.

Damn it.

Mr. Schumer was right. Graham was too busy checking out Emily to realize she was trying to pay for the six-pack. He pulled out his wallet. "Here, I've got this."

Emily frowned. "But it was my idea—"

Mr. Schumer thrust her license and credit card at her. Then he looked Graham right in the eye. "I'm gonna need to see some ID."

"You're kidding me."

The old man tried to stare him down.

Graham tried not to show his amusement as he took out his driver's license. "You really think I'm younger than she is? Two years younger than she is?"

"We got laws. No ID, no alcohol."

Graham tossed his driver's license on the counter.

"Illinois, is it?" Mr. Schumer held it up, comparing the photo to Graham's face like it was a wanted poster, not a driver's license. Then he blatantly started reading everything on the license, not just the birth year. "Six-one, green eyes." He stopped to scrutinize Graham's eyes, as if he'd lie about such a thing. "Chicago. Seems like a long ways from here. Tell me, son. You came all the way from Chicago just to buy some beer?"

Graham flicked the credit card in his hand like it was a playing card, then held it out between two fingers for the man to take. "Yes, I did."

The way Emily smothered her laughter nearly made Graham lose his poker face, but after another brief stare down, Mr. Schumer conceded and slid the six-pack over the bar code scanner. He turned his attention back to Emily. "How's your mama?"

"She's fine, thank you for asking."

"She sure is proud of your schooling. Told me you're getting honors at Oklahoma Tech. She says you're going straight through to get a master's degree. Not this June but next, you'll have your MBA. How about that? Your mama's gonna throw a party like you've never seen when you graduate, you wait and see. If she doesn't, I'll be as surprised as a pup with his first porcupine."

Graham was amused, until he realized Emily was not.

Mr. Schumer talked on. "You'll be running Wall Street in no time. Don't forget us little people when you're living in your penthouse apartment."

"Yessir."

The country version of *Yes, sir* was the shortest answer he'd heard Emily give all night. Clearly, she did not want to discuss this. Graham signed his name on the credit card machine's screen so he could get her out of here.

"I don't know what your plans are for the rest of the night, young lady, but stay away from Keller's Bar. My police scanner's been blowing up with all the goings-on over there."

"Have they called any ambulances out?" Emily asked, suddenly alert and interested. "Was anyone shot?"

"Nobody's shot anybody, and don't you think for one second about running over there like you're some kind of Texas Rescue hero. A pretty young thing like you has no business being around a crime scene at this hour of the night. Not at any hour of the day, neither."

"Actually, I'm certified in first aid by Texas Rescue." Her teacher voice was back, patient but firm. "If I was closer than the ambulances, what kind of person would I be if I didn't try to help until they showed up?"

Graham thought she made an excellent point, but it wasn't in Mr. Schumer to concede.

"Hmpf. It's after dark. There's men who know first aid, too. You let them handle things."

Emily kept her chin up, her voice calm, but her eyes narrowed as she took aim. "You know my family. Don't you think my mama raised me not to turn my back when someone needs help?"

She shoots; she scores.

Mr. Schumer shifted on his stool, uncomfortable. "Like I said, no one got shot. They're not calling in the medevac helicopters. If the men who were fighting can't handle their own black eyes and broken ribs, then it's past time they learned how. You and Benjamin go enjoy the rest of your evening somewhere else."

Benjamin startled Emily for a second, Graham could tell. She took the six-pack and said good-night as she headed for the door. Graham took his credit card back.

"I mean it now," Mr. Schumer said to him, looking ready for a man-to-man chat now that Emily had walked away. "That's not a situation fit for any girl, no matter what she thinks. Nothing but trouble."

Poor Emily. Mr. Schumer wasn't ever going to see her

as anything but a little girl. Graham suspected she knew it, with her *yessir* and the way she'd walked away. She stood with her hand on the glass door, waiting for him.

"I don't want to see Emily in any kind of trouble," Mr. Schumer persisted.

It was kind of sweet, the way the old man looked out for his granddaughter's friend. Very small town. Graham slid the credit card into his wallet. "We'll steer clear of the bar. Good night."

"Any kind of trouble, son. You catch my meaning?"

Graham hesitated in the middle of putting his wallet in his pocket and turned back to the glowering grandpa.

"I see the way you're looking at her, Chicago. I know what it's like to be young, but there's no reason to get a young lady in trouble. If you need something, I've got it right here behind the counter."

He couldn't be—but yes, he was. The old man was offering him condoms.

"I don't ask questions," the old man said, deadly serious, "and I won't tell your parents a thing about it. Ever."

Graham drew a blank. He couldn't even picture his father getting a phone call informing him that his thirty-year-old military-veteran son had purchased a box of condoms.

"I know folks say wait, wait, wait, but there hasn't been a generation yet that does that. Not back in my day. Not back in my grandfather's day. There's always been babies born six or seven months after the wedding. Everyone's family Bible has one of those. Instead of giving you a lecture that you aren't going to listen to anyway, I'd rather see you young people just buy what you need to buy in order to stay out of trouble."

Graham would have thought he was in some 1950s television show, except the world was in color instead of black and white. "I understand." That seemed neutral enough.

"Good." The old man started to reach under the counter.

"No." Graham held out his hand to stop him, exasperated. "No, thanks."

"You sure about that?"

Which, of course, made Graham pause to consider whether or not he really had a condom at hand. He had two seabags in his SUV, all the clothes he'd need for three months of hay and horses. He'd stopped at a big box store on his way through Dallas to buy a comforter and some towels when Uncle Gus had belatedly mentioned that the bunkhouse provided the bed and mattress but only the bed and mattress. But somewhere in his shaving kit, Graham had condoms. He was pretty sure.

"Because a girl like Emily, she's not sticking around here. Her mama's got plans for her. She doesn't need to get saddled down with housework and a husband and a baby."

Never would Graham have guessed that tonight would be the night he got a lecture on safe sex from a gas station owner. If he wasn't so surprised, he'd laugh. He glanced over to Emily. Judging by the look on her face, if she couldn't hear every word, she could hear enough.

Emily was not amused.

This might be a small-town novelty to him, something he could laugh about from a distance, but Emily lived here. Having this store owner make assumptions about her sex life—about her entire life—was intrusive. Having someone else's grandfather decide for her that she needed birth control, then deciding what kind she needed…

Yeah, Graham was not amused, either. Not anymore.

Mr. Schumer pulled out a little black box and tapped it on the counter. "I'd hate to see her—"

"I get that." Graham knew the old-timer thought he was being helpful, but he was also being a patronizing son of a brick, and he'd already been told *no* once. It was time for a different type of man-to-man conversation. Graham kept his voice low, his words meant for Schumer, not Emily. "I also get that you're helping yourself to a whole lot of assumptions about me and more about Emily. You may have read my mind—"

"Hmpf."

"But you haven't read hers. She knows her own mind. She calls her own shots. You're assuming she can't control herself if she's alone with me, and that is an insult. Back in your day and back in your grandfather's day, a man wouldn't put up with another man insulting his date like that." Where that old-fashioned notion had come from, Graham couldn't say, but it seemed to strike a chord with Mr. Schumer.

Mr. Schumer glanced toward the door and immediately away, not quite able to look at Emily, but Graham he scrutinized for a moment longer. "I guess you two aren't kids."

Graham said nothing.

Mr. Schumer finally nodded to himself, and he put the box back under the counter. "You come back at lunch one day, when there's brisket."

Graham accepted that concession with a nod of his own. "I'll do that."

As he walked toward Emily, she leaned back against the door, opening it so he could walk right through, but he slipped his arm under the coat and around her waist, and he left with her by his side, ruffles tickling the inside of his wrist.

He couldn't decipher the way she was looking at him as he took the six-pack from her and opened the passenger door. She was thoughtful, or maybe amused. Bemused, he decided.

He nearly dropped a kiss on her lips. "Is Mr. Schumer watching us?"

"Every move."

"Tell me getting a drink like the locals doesn't involve sitting in this parking lot and having a beer while Mr. Schumer chaperones."

"Not with an SUV like yours, it doesn't. We can go somewhere much nicer. It's just a little farther down the road."

Graham got behind the wheel, and when she pointed him west, deeper into ranch country, neither one of them looked back at the horizon to see if the red and blue lights were still keeping them together.

Chapter Six

"I couldn't hear every word in there, but I think you just defended my honor."

Since Emily was turned toward Graham, watching his profile as he drove, she saw the way his mouth quirked in a fleeting smile before he turned stoic once more in the dashboard lights.

"Thank you," she said simply.

He glanced at her, back to the black road. "I wouldn't normally face off with an old man like that. I just didn't like the way he assumed you were some kind of... I don't know, some kind of nymphomaniac."

So you set him straight. She hadn't had to defend herself—not even in her own head, which was what she did pretty often when the argument got hopeless. Instead, she'd leaned against that glass door, surprised at the turn the conversation had taken, what she could hear of it. Then *not* surprised. This was Graham, after all, a man who wouldn't leave her behind. He wouldn't let her reputation twist in the wind, either. This was a great night; she absolutely loved every minute she spent with him.

So she smiled. "I don't know, maybe you should have bought what he was selling. How do you know I'm not a nymphomaniac?"

The lift of his eyebrow told her just how absurd he found that possibility, but then those deliciously male, surprisingly soft lips quirked again before he said, with perfect seriousness, "If you really were a nymphomaniac, I wouldn't have had to buy anything, either. I'd expect you to pull a whole strip of condoms out of your little cowboy boot. So far, I've just seen a key and a driver's license."

"So far." She slid her fingers over her bare knee, down inside her boot, inching down her shin, until Graham tore his eyes off the road to scowl at her hand.

She pulled her hand out and wiggled her fingers. "Kidding. Definitely not a nymphomaniac. Had you worried there for a minute, didn't I?"

"I don't know if *worried* is exactly the right term."

"Hopeful?"

He kept one hand on the steering wheel and rubbed his neck with the other, still frowning.

"Confused?" she suggested.

"Let's go with that."

"Slow down here. There's going to be a break in the fence—there it is. Since we've already put a little mud on the tires, we can do some cross-country driving to go to Old Man Cooper's farm. It used to be one of my very favorite places. It's probably all overgrown now, but there used to be a trail back here...oh."

The trail was not only there, but it had been upgraded to a dirt road, cut through brush and grasses that looked like the walls of a tunnel in the headlights. They followed it until it opened into a clearing. There, perfectly still in the moonlight, was a small lake.

"My lake," she said softly, wondering why she was surprised it was still here—wondering why she felt like crying. "You should turn off your headlights so you can see the moon on the water."

Graham pulled closer to the lake, parking where a lot of previous cars had already flattened the ground. He turned off the lights.

"Isn't it pretty?" she asked.

Lights suddenly came on across the water, the headlights of a pickup truck that backed up so fast, so hard, it churned up dirt.

Emily shut her eyes and turned her face away. "Jeez, someone has to be home by midnight." She waited until she could see in the night once more. It was little for a lake, but definitely more than a pond. The moonlight was white on its black surface. "Okay, *now* isn't it pretty?"

Graham was watching the pickup truck as it left, always the alert bodyguard.

Emily sighed for him, but Graham shook his head and actually chuckled. "Is this the local make-out place? Lover's Lane for teenagers?"

He was laughing at her pond. Her lake.

And here she'd been feeling sorry for him. She glared at him instead. "No."

Graham gave her that skeptical raised eyebrow again.

"Not really. Not always."

"Either you park here to kiss a girl without adult supervision, or you don't."

"Fine. Then I guess it was the local make-out place. But it was more than that. I always thought it was so pretty."

Graham had probably been around the world with the military. He'd probably seen incredible sights like oceans and waterfalls. She'd only seen Austin and San Antonio—and more than enough of Oklahoma.

She let go of her indignation. "It's just a pond, I know. Don't laugh at me."

"I'm not. I'm just feeling…old. It's been a very long time since I drove a girl to a place like this."

"I know what you mean. The last time I was here, I was fifteen. Seven years ago. I kind of thought it would be abandoned and all overgrown by now. I don't know why I thought that. Just because I could no longer come here, that doesn't mean no one else would come here."

She wasn't the center of the universe. She knew that, of course. But she was looking at a lake that proved life went on without her. This piece of her youth belonged to other people now, people who'd never heard of her, people who didn't care if she'd ever been here before them.

She felt a moment of vertigo.

Graham's voice anchored her in the here and now. "Why didn't you come here when you were sixteen or seventeen?"

"We moved back to San Antonio my junior year. Then Mom got remarried and we moved back here my senior year, but my new stepfather didn't believe in free time. Or in dating. My big freedom was sleeping over at my aunt and uncle's. I spent every minute at their place riding. I missed the horses more than I missed this lake, I suppose." She couldn't get enough of the view now, though, as the breeze rippled the reflected moonlight. "Maybe since my memories kind of faded away, I thought this place would, too. It's all so vivid now."

"Teenagers wouldn't abandon a place like this." Graham sounded kind again, that gentleness back in his deep voice. "Especially when it's this pretty."

"This really wasn't just a make-out place. We'd lie out

on blankets and stare at the stars and talk about all our plans for the future and how great our lives were going to be. If you didn't have too much ranch work on a Sunday, you could come in the afternoon to swim. I had the idea to start building a dock the summer I was fifteen. Mr. Cooper didn't care what we did as long as we didn't leave empty beer bottles or leave a fire burning." The memories were sweet, but this place was no longer hers. That innocence was over, and never would be hers again.

She couldn't look at the lake, not while she was drowning in this surge of memories, so she looked at Graham. "Sorry. I didn't realize I'd feel so strange. I think I'm suffering from a bad case of nostalgia. When did I get old enough to have nostalgic memories of my childhood?" She rubbed her fingers over her chest, right where her heart hurt. "It sucks. Yay, adulthood. Rah, rah, rah."

Graham didn't say anything.

She wrinkled her nose apologetically. "Sorry. Nostalgia's not very sexy, is it?"

Graham looked at her for the longest time. When he raised his hand, she thought he was going to touch her, maybe slide his hand under her hair again, reaching across this extra-wide center console that kept them so far apart.

Instead, he pointed out the window. "Looks like someone finished your dock for you."

Emily had to sit up tall to get her eyes at the same height as his, so she could see over the pond grasses. There, in the moonlight, was a completed dock, a little run of twelve feet or so, just out to where she knew the water got really deep, deep enough to dive in.

"They did it." She imagined other kids working on it, kids like the younger version of herself, fifteen and certain she could make the world work just the way she wanted it to. That hadn't worked out so far, but maybe it would for other kids. "Good for them. I like the idea that more girls like me are out there."

"Boys might have built it, too."

She dismissed his dry observation with a flick of her fingers. "The only reason the boys ever helped is because the girls were working on it first. We designed it. We got the boards and nails. But we were very concerned about our tan lines, you know, so we all thought the best thing to wear for hammering boards on a hot Sunday afternoon was a bathing suit. That's when boys started showing up."

"I stand corrected. That's entirely plausible."

"You wouldn't believe how easy it is to get a boy to do what you want when you're wearing a bikini top and cut-off short-shorts."

A small pause. "I'd believe it."

She smiled at the memory. "I suspect girls in bikinis are behind a whole lot of industrious males."

Graham laughed, outright laughed, and Emily turned toward him to laugh, too, but her breath caught in her chest. He looked so good, her handsome and buff body-guard, when he was off duty and carefree. Almost as good as he looked after he kissed her.

I want him. I want to see him happy. I want to be the reason he's happy.

She had another moment of vertigo, another emotion catching her by surprise, another change in where she saw herself in the world. Her dream of owning a ranch suddenly looked different; a man got painted into the picture. A lover, a friend. Of course—how had she thought it would be better to be on her own?

It was scary. Too much, too big of a change.

Graham opened his door. "Let's go see how they did."

The cold air came inside and brushed her cheeks, but her body was warm in his coat. He was going to be cold, though. Maybe he had another coat or a blanket or some-thing. She turned to look in the back seat—two more bucket seats and another wide console separating them.

"What are you looking for?" he asked.

"You know, for parking at a make-out place, all this roomy luxury sucks. Not one bench seat. Just this mile-wide center barricade. Mr. Schumer would approve."

At his silence, she looked up to find that he was lean-ing over the console, too, looking at the back seats with her. Their faces were so close—and his looked distinctly amused.

"Those seats recline," he said. "Fully."

"Ah."

"A footrest comes up, so you can stretch out. It's pretty luxurious."

"I see."

"Are we done with the backseat recon?"

"I was looking for—never mind." She kissed him. Full on, mouth on mouth. His lips were so soft. The shadow of his beard was rough on her palm as she ran her hand along his jaw before burying her hand in his hair. She held his head firmly as she changed the angle of the kiss, leaning into him as she leaned a little farther across the console.

He let her control the kiss. When she nudged his lips apart with her own, he obeyed. When she nipped his lower lip, when she licked his upper lip, when she cupped his jaw in her two hands, he let her come closer and closer, inching his head back as she turned into him, her knee on her seat now for leverage as she pushed him back into his seat with kiss after kiss.

He took over, and he wanted to taste her. She wanted to let him. Without breaking off the kiss, he slid his hands under the coat, up her sides, and lifted her up and over the console, turning her so that she was lying in his lap, cradled in his arms, her legs draped across the console, her boots on the passenger seat. The coat was still wrapped around her, but she shivered, anyway, a physical thrill at how strong he was to be able to lift her so easily. He kept her close to his chest with one arm as he reached for the open door and slammed it shut.

And then, oh then, he really kissed her—her cheeks, her eyelids, her forehead. Not little butterfly kisses, but passionate ones, like he was claiming her, every inch of her skin. He turned her head away with one hand and kissed her throat, then under her jaw, then her chin, then turned her head back to take her mouth. She'd never felt this before, never been kissed like this before. She could hardly think, but she knew that this, *this*, was being ravished.

And she loved it. She lay boneless in his strong arms, letting him show her just how much he wanted her, proving to her how much he could make her want him. His mouth returned to hers over and over, tasting her, then exploring her more slowly, but not gently. It was physical. It was carnal. He kissed her with intent. He kissed her like he owned her.

He didn't want to stop. She knew that like she knew her own thoughts, but he lifted his lips from hers. A pause, another taste. Over her mouth, he growled a demand. "Now take it back."

"Take…" It was hard to speak. "Take what back?"

"You said my car was no good for making out."

"Oh…ah…"

"Still think it sucks?"

But then she felt him smiling against her mouth. That smile was so intimate, coming from someone so stern and strong, she felt it all the way to her heart. *My private bodyguard smile.* She wanted to smile back, but she could hardly breathe. She couldn't even keep her eyes open.

The coat she wore like a cape was still mostly around her, but without taking his smile away from her lips, she felt Graham very deliberately lift the edge of the coat and peel it away, laying it open. Her blue dress covered her up to the base of her throat, yet she felt so exposed, wildly aware that his hand had let go of the coat. She could hardly stand the anticipation. Where was his hand? Where would he touch her?

His mouth closed over hers again as his whole hand, warm and large, wrapped around her side, just below her breast. She arched her back, hoping his hand would move just a bit higher, but instead he smoothed his way lower, to the soft indent of her waist, over the firm curve of her hip, to the edge of her dress. His hand was warm on her bare thigh as he slid his palm to the back of her leg, then lifted her knee slightly, holding her there a moment, letting his hand warm the sensitive area behind her knee. Oh, she hadn't known she was sensitive behind her knee. She was dying, melting, completely undone by this man who so very clearly, so very incredibly, knew what he was doing.

He demanded, with a gentle bite on her lower lip, that she pay attention to the kiss again. She tried to focus on his mouth, until his hand lifted from her leg, leaving her skin cool in the air. He was going to touch her body somewhere else, any second...

She was practically lapping up his every kiss when his hand returned to her side, tightening around her ribs as he lifted her, shifted her with that one strong hand so more of her weight was cradled in his other arm. She was aching for his touch, and this time, he slid upward, ruffles slipping under his hand as he brushed the side of her breast, then rested there for a moment.

She made some sort of incoherent sound, and she felt him smile against her lips again, but this time it was more tender than devilish. He whispered something serious against her lips as he firmly ran his thumb over her nipple. She gasped at the sensation. He kissed her hard again and cupped her entire breast, shaping the softness to fill his hand.

"Graham—please—". Words were hard, so hard when her body was ruling her mind. "You have protection for us." It wasn't a question. It was a demand. It was time.

Graham devoured her, working his way to the soft spot below her ear. "We can take this all the way to the end." She wasn't sure if that was a question, either, when the answer was obvious. She was putty in his hands, writhing with want under his touch. She wanted to make love to him, she wanted to be part of him, with an intensity that overwhelmed every other thought.

He slid his hand with a sure touch down her side, her hip, her thigh, and then under the hem of her dress. The back of his hand grazed up her inner thigh, then over her most sensitive spot, knuckles smoothing over the slippery nylon of her underwear.

She was not going to last. There was no way she could wait for him if he kept touching her there. She would climax— then his thumb pressed over just the right spot, drawing deliberate circles over the smooth fabric, and she realized that was exactly what he wanted her to do. The firm pressure of his thumb became the firmer pressure of his hand, and she was lost, the burst of pleasure blotting out the world.

Chapter Seven

His heart hurt.

It shouldn't.

A beautiful woman was draped across Graham's lap, her legs smooth and shapely, stretched across the width of his front seats, her feet hidden in cowgirl boots. A beautiful, *satisfied* cowgirl, whom he'd just sent over the edge with the weight of his hand on her feminine, incredible, absolutely spectacular body. She was panting gently, eyes closed, coming down from her high, coming back to this moment.

Coming back to him.

Why did that make his heart hurt?

Of course his body hurt. His hands, his mouth, his eyes had all been roaming over the richness that was Emily, getting their fill of her shape, her taste, her beauty. Their greed caused an arousal so complete, even his shirt felt like too much on his skin. The unforgiving denim of his jeans caused outright pain. Every part of his body wanted to be in contact with every part of hers. But while he watched Emily catch her breath, his heart was pounding with more than just sexual desire.

This is special. This is different.

It couldn't be. He wasn't ready for that.

He'd never be ready for that. His life had veered too far from that, too long ago. But Emily sure as hell was no last cigarette. She wasn't just a woman, or the first woman he'd had in ages, or the last woman he'd have for a long while.

Emily was a whole new addiction.

She was holding on to a fistful of his shirt. He watched her fingers relax, and then with a shivery breath, she opened her eyes and blinked at him, slow and sleepy, as the moonlight poured in through the windshield.

She smiled.

This one. She's the one.

He rejected the thought harshly. But damn, she was special. He looked away, down that river of blue ruffles.

She slipped her fingers under his shirtsleeve, traveling a little way from his wrist to the crease of his elbow, making the rest of his skin jealous of that little piece of his arm.

"You're still totally dressed," she said.

"So are you."

"I am?" Her laugh was languid, lazy. "I am. How is that even possible? I don't feel dressed. I feel like I've been... uncovered."

His heart, it hurt.

She slipped her hand down his wrist and slid her fingers between his, holding his hand as she turned thoughtful, a little serious, frowning slightly. "I feel a little exposed. I should be blushing."

"You weren't, and you shouldn't."

She held on to his shoulder to pull herself upright, so she was sitting sideways on his lap. "I shouldn't?"

Graham started to shake his head, but Emily's frown was already giving way to another smile. It started small, coy, but quickly turned into a laugh, all joy.

"Then I won't." She leaned forward, just to touch noses with him. "I can't wait to do that again. Let's be naked this time."

Hell, yeah. All the blood in his body went south, leaving his brain empty, just empty. Graham thunked his head back on the headrest.

She began placing little kisses along his jaw. He regained enough brainpower to comprehend that much. She put both hands on his shoulders as she got to her knees, dragging one knee across his lap, grazing his aching hardness, so that she was straddling him as she knelt over him in the driver's seat, pressed close to him by the steering wheel at her back. Her long hair fell forward to brush his face as she bent over him, kissing, kissing.

"Emily." He tried to say it firmly. It came out as a growl.

Her hands slipped between them. The awkward angle didn't prevent her from unbuckling his belt and the top button of his jeans. The relief that the extra room gave his body was short-lived, because her hands brushing so near drove his hardness to its limit. He grabbed her wrists. "Emily. Stop."

She rocked her body against his. He closed his eyes against the bright flare of pleasure. She would be heaven in bed. Bright heaven.

"Stop, sweetheart." He was murmuring the words like a lover, between the kisses he was returning. He let go of her wrists and slid his fingers between hers, holding both of her hands. "Hey. Slow down a moment, beautiful." Not effective, either.

Emily will be hurt when you leave her behind, hurt worse than any bar fight.

That grim reality put the right tone in his voice. "We need to stop now."

She sat back just a few inches to see his face better. He liked the way she looked him in the eye, even when she was confused. Of course he liked it. He liked every single thing about this woman.

"Why?" she said, a gently spoken word, a simple curiosity.

Because if I have you once, I'll never stop craving you.

No—this was about her, not about him, but damn, that thought had been too clear.

"Because I'm leaving, remember? I have to leave." He could see it in her eyes when his words started to penetrate.

"But...you're passing through. You could stay a few days first? The weekend?"

A sex-drenched weekend, just Emily on the white sheets of a hotel bed. The image must have been in her mind as well, for she leaned into him, slid up the hard length of him, and whispered in his ear. "Stay the weekend."

He forced his brain to keep functioning when his body wanted to shut it down. It was a learned skill, one taught from the first day in the military, how to overrule physical needs, how to complete a mission while the body clamored for essentials like food and sleep. Sex with Emily felt like just such an essential. He overruled his body now, no matter how tempting it was to just shut off his brain and let his body have what it needed. Emily would satisfy him, Emily *wanted* to satisfy him and herself, too, but he remembered who he was, where he'd been, where he was going. He didn't belong with joy and beauty.

He held her still with one hand on her hip, warm under the coat. The other hand he used to cup her face, so they were looking eye to eye and he had her full attention. "I'll be gone at dawn."

That stilled her in a way his hands could not.

"I'm sorry, Emily. Sorrier than I can say." He'd killed the last trace of her smile. "This was supposed to be just a kiss at your old make-out spot. A fun little dare when you said the front seat wouldn't work."

"Or the back seat." She dropped her gaze to his chest, so he saw only her lashes.

"Or the back seat. It's a kiss that got out of control. I went too far, too fast, but I've got to put the brakes on. I can't—I can't be your lover and stay."

She looked so sad with her eyes downcast like that, as if he was rejecting her, when he was actually refusing to treat her as no more than a casual lay.

"Look at me, Emily. I can't be your lover and stay, and I can't be your lover and leave, either. I'm not going to have sex with you while a steering wheel's at your back and then just drop you off in a bar parking lot and drive away. I won't do that."

"Just a kiss," she repeated, stuck at the beginning of his explanation.

He hoped the rest of his words would stick with her, too. He hoped she'd see that she was more special to him than a kiss or a dare.

"Look, I need to cool off," she said. "So, I'll just—um—"

She tried to get off his lap, but that straddle position that she'd settled into with such confidence now made for awkward movements. The bucket seat that had felt like such bliss was too tight for the two of them to get untangled with any grace. Emily reached behind her right hip, groping for the door's handle, until it opened and a rush of warm air escaped. She escaped, too. Or rather, she climbed off him and jumped the step to the ground, grabbing at his coat to keep it around her shoulders, grabbing at her hem to tug her dress back into place.

He followed before she could shut the door. Out in the cold, he rebuttoned his jeans, rebuckled his belt angrily, mad at himself for how far he'd let things go. He stood beside her, letting the air do what it could to chill their passion.

"I'm just going to go for a little walk and check out the pond." Emily pulled his coat more tightly around herself and gave him a brave little laugh. "It's kind of been a theme tonight."

"I'll walk with you."

She shied away from him, just a little duck of her chin and a turn of a colder shoulder. He felt it. He deserved it. She was hurt that he'd turned her down, but tomorrow would come, and Emily had a whole lot of tomorrows ahead of her. For all of those tomorrows, she'd be glad that she wouldn't look back on this night and feel like she'd been used by a guy who'd only stopped in her town for a drink.

"Do you have another coat for yourself?" she asked.

She was going to let him walk with her, then. He was glad. Grateful, even. In silence, she followed him to the back of the SUV. He lifted the rear door to the cargo area. In the harsh white of the interior LED lights, he pushed aside the tumbled new bedding and the towels with their price tags still attached, no longer a neatly folded stack after their jolting cross-country drive. His two Marine Corps seabags were still lined up and tied down, exactly as he'd loaded them back in Chicago. The silence was going on too long; when he opened the metal clasp at the top of one olive drab bag, it sounded loud.

Emily trailed her fingers over the stenciled name on the bottom of the other bag. "These duffel bags look like the real deal."

He was glad to hear her voice. "We call them seabags, but yeah. I've had them a long time."

"Seabags. Were you in the Navy?"

"Marines. Oo-rah."

It was the default response in the Marine Corps for nearly any kind of comment, said far more frequently than the motto, *Semper fi.* He said the *oo-rah* quietly, tongue in cheek, as he watched her, unsure, for once, how to decipher the expression on her face. He pulled out the olive drab track jacket he knew would be near the top of the seabag, rolled in accordance with regulation. Some of the Marine lessons were worth following still; rolled items were the most efficient way to pack a duffel bag. Once a Marine, always a Marine, as the saying went. *Semper fi.*

Emily ran her fingers over the block letters he'd stenciled so many years ago during his very first week as an officer: GRAHAM, B.

"Benjamin," she said softly.

"Yes."

"I almost slept with a man who'd only given me his last name." She didn't make it sound like that was a good thing. "Mr. Schumer knew your first name before I did. Why did you tell me your name was Graham?"

"My name *is* Graham."

"With everybody?"

Why did she seem upset about this? "All the time. Always has been. Midshipman Graham, Lieutenant Graham, Captain Graham. In the corporate world, my assistant put calls through to Mr. Graham. Graham takes clients to dinner. Graham buys a round of cigars on the golf course. And when someone new introduces herself to me, I shake the hand she offers and introduce myself as Graham."

"Like a business acquaintance?"

"I'm not sure what you're asking."

Whatever she was asking, it was enough to make Emily drop that arm's distance she'd been maintaining. She came a step closer to him, and she lifted her chin to a challenging angle. He preferred it over that shy duck-away.

"I'm asking what name you go by with the women who know you better than I do. The women whom you *are* willing to take to bed? In the dark, what name is a woman supposed to cry out at that moment? Do the privileged few know Benjamin?"

There were no other women he was more willing to take to bed than her. That wasn't it at all. He just didn't want to use her and leave her. If he and Emily could've stayed in bed for a weekend—for a year—forever—

He had to stop that train of thought. Keep it light.

"My mother calls me Benjamin. I don't think that would be the best thing to hear at that moment, do you?"

But Emily didn't smile with him. She looked away and traced the letter *B* with one finger. He dared to touch her again. He had never *wanted* to stop touching her, but maybe he hadn't made that clear. She inhaled sharply when he slid his hand under her hair to the back of her neck, but he pulled her close, anyway.

"The only woman who matters at all to me has been calling me Graham all night. I was not keeping you at a distance by giving you that name, not at any distance whatsoever, but if you want to call me Benjamin, go ahead. Ben works, too. I'm not a fan of Benji."

Now her expression was easy to read. She was deciding whether or not to believe him. He waited, pressing his fingers in slow, lazy circles on the back of her neck to relieve the tension there.

"I'm not a fan of Emmie," she said. "Em if you must. But really, the whole three syllables isn't a lot to ask of a man."

"Emily."

"Benjamin." She thought it over. Her expression said she didn't like it. "Maybe Ben. Hello, Ben."

"Hello."

Then she threw up a hand. "Oh, to heck with it. Graham. It's going to have to be Graham, like a business deal. You know, when a man gives you an amazing orgasm as Graham, he's pretty much going to be stuck as Graham in your mind forever after that. 'Me and Graham, at the lake that night.' That's just the way it is."

There was a whole lot to process in that declaration. The fact that he was going to be in her mind forever tugged at his heart, because he already knew she was going to be the standard by which he measured any other evening with any other woman from this day on. But the most important thing was that she'd returned to her bold and straightforward style. He was so relieved, he wanted to laugh and kiss her and thank her for still talking to him, all at the same time.

He went with the kiss.

He felt her soften, felt her give in, but then she backed out of his hold. She was better than he was at resisting this new addiction.

She'd been wearing his coat as a cape all night, but now she put her arms through the sleeves. He put on the track jacket, a uniform item that Marines were allowed to wear as civilian dress. He could wear it even though he was no longer in the military. Out of habit, he zipped it up halfway. Regulation.

Emily tugged on his sleeve. "This is all I was looking for in the back seat. Something to keep you warm while we went to look at the dock. Pretty innocent of me. But then I started kissing you. I know that I was the one who started kissing you first—"

"Nothing is your fault. You didn't start it."

She let go of his sleeve and shoved her fists in the coat pockets. "Actually, I did. I introduced myself to you at Keller's. I offered to buy you a drink. Later on, I practically begged you to kiss me on the side of the road, and I brought you here. But you..." She fell silent.

He was keenly interested to hear where this was going. "But I...?"

"You're a grown man, Graham. I mean that in the best way. You know exactly what you're doing."

Well, he had known, until he'd met her and gotten the crazy idea that he could enjoy a few harmless hours dancing or drinking with her, then walk away unaffected.

"In the front seat... I've never been kissed like that before. I've never been touched so perfectly..." She blushed now in a way she hadn't blushed in the front seat. "I've never been touched so perfectly *accurately* before."

Ah—she meant that kind of knowing what he was doing. It was tough not to feel a little smug about that. Hard on the heels of that thought was jealousy at the idea of other men touching her, followed by the even more irrational anger that other men had apparently fumbled around and not pleased her. They didn't deserve to touch her if they couldn't please her. Scratch that—no one deserved to touch her. Ever. Graham could break every man who'd ever dared to try.

Addicts were irrational.

Emily's blush didn't stop her from being bold. "To be

perfectly honest, I loved it, Graham. Every moment of it. I want more of you."

Hell, yeah. But he beat down the impulse. She was too young for him, too full of life, too everything as she blushed, pink-cheeked in the pool of artificial light. But she was a hella-brave woman—she never dropped her gaze despite her blush.

In fact, she was studying him closely. "You're choosing to bring it all from a full gallop to a hard stop. That's not my first choice, but it takes two. You said it best. It wouldn't be any fun if one of us wasn't having any fun."

It would be fun, no doubt, but her regrets afterward wouldn't be. Didn't she understand this was all for her sake?

"But I don't like the way you're making this all about me," she said, echoing his thought with her own kind of accuracy. "You're being some kind of noble Sir Galahad, protecting my delicate sensibilities. I didn't ask you to do that. If we've come up to a line that you don't want to cross, I can respect that, Graham, I really can. But don't cast me in the role of some virginal princess who is too delicate to watch you drive away in the morning. The real reason we aren't making love right this second is because *you* don't want to cross that line."

She squinted at the light in the ceiling of the cargo area as she reached up to find the switch. She turned it off. The darkness was a relief.

The silence was not, but damn if Graham could think of the right thing to say. Of anything to say. He could only watch Emily become more vivid as his eyes adjusted to the moonlight.

She stepped close to him, as close as she'd been when she'd put her hand on his heart and asked him for that first kiss. *Graham, it's cold out.*

She was right. She had taken the initiative—brave, bold Emily. The piece of him that would always be a Marine Corps officer valued that. She had everything a man could want in a teammate: initiative, a cool head, the ability to adjust when plans went awry. She kept a sense of humor; she smiled easily and often. Add to that her beauty, her body, the way she'd be heaven in bed, and Graham knew he was looking at the one woman for him—or the woman that would have been perfect for the younger version of himself, the Ben Graham who had existed once upon a time.

He'd met her too late.

He was done. Burned out. But if he'd met her years ago, if he'd been the one who was just finishing college, the one who didn't know what lay ahead, if he'd been the one who was twenty-two—

She would have been fourteen.

He would have already finished his first year as a lieutenant in the Marines, and she would have been a high school freshman who could have had no more than a crush on him. No matter how kind he would've tried to be if she'd followed him around, her young heart would have inevitably been crushed. He would've been her first disappointment, her first disillusionment.

With one hand, he gently tucked her hair behind her ear. *I'm sorry, sweet girl, but I'm not the right man for you. Someday, you'll fall in love with someone your own age, and you'll see what I mean. I promise.*

She closed her eyes briefly and leaned her cheek into his touch. "I guess I'm wondering what you think will happen if we cross that line."

"I don't want any hearts to break."

But Emily stepped into him, arms around his neck, fingers in his hair. She fit herself against him, woman to man, breast to chest and softness to hardness. Graham wasn't twenty-two; she was. Twenty-two and grown-up and absolutely spectacular.

Graham bent his head and took her mouth with his, claiming her as if he could keep her.

And then he let her go.

Chapter Eight

The dock made her angry.

It was well built, sturdy, exactly what Emily had had in mind when she'd started it seven years ago. She doubted she could have made it come out this well. Not at fifteen. This dock had been built by adults, someone with construction connections who could sink proper footings. Someone had even replaced the old rope that had once hung from a branch over the water. The new rope dangled down to brush the end of the dock.

When no dock had existed, the old rope had been harder to reach, but they'd always managed, standing on shoulders or climbing the tree. Then they'd dared each other to swing out over the water and perform tricks in the air before hitting the surface, stupid and frankly dangerous somersaults and midair cartwheels. The new rope was better, thick and unfrayed, and it had knots tied at intervals to make grips for hands and summertime bare feet. No one would slide down this new rope very far if their grip slipped. No one would get a rope burn so deep it drew blood.

No one would learn a hard lesson on how to keep a good grip, either.

She sounded like a crusty old grandpa, like Mr. Schumer on a good day. Sexual frustration made her grouchy. She hadn't known that. She hadn't ever wanted a man the way she wanted Graham.

Emily reached up high with one hand to grip the rope and test her weight on it. With the edges of her boots standing on the bottom knot, she bounced the branch a few times. Definitely a better rope than hers had been, despite the wimpy knots. It ticked her off, this proof that her way had been the wrong way, too headstrong, inadequate.

Graham was standing at the shore, watching her in the dark. Always on alert, always the bodyguard. For some reason, he'd stopped at the edge of the lake, though, and just nodded at the dock and told her to go ahead and check it out. She supposed he was trying to give her space to indulge her memories. She would have preferred to indulge in the oblivion she'd felt in his arms, cradled to his chest, when the only thing she'd needed had been more of his touch. What would it be like to make him focus on her touch that way? What would it be like to have his body all to herself, all hers to touch and learn and love on and—

Her hand slipped down the rope.

She caught herself on a knot.

That only made her angrier. The dock was just a few inches below her feet, but the safety knot made her feel like she was in danger when she wasn't. It was all safe now, standard rope, standard dock. She looked across the dark water, trying to remember the lake the wild way it had been at fifteen.

She remembered how she'd been at fifteen. Fearless—

she'd dreamed of owning her own cattle ranch. Not a cute little hobby farm with twenty head of dairy cows, but a real cattle operation like Uncle James and Aunt Jessie owned. Of course, even at fifteen she'd known that would take millions of dollars if enough land ever came up for sale. Almost all cattle ranches were either inherited legacies or corporate holdings. Uncle James had inherited his ranch.

At fifteen, Emily had understood that Uncle James was her uncle by marriage. Her aunt had married the owner of the James Hill Ranch. Emily never had been and never would be in line to inherit anything, but it was still the family ranch. Uncle James and Aunt Jessie's two boys were her first cousins, and she'd grown up with them, always trying to keep up with them. Considering Trey and Luke were older and bigger, she'd done pretty well just by never giving up. *Stubborn since the day she was born*, that was what her mother and Aunt Jessie would say.

There wasn't another James Hill out there to inherit or purchase that she knew of, but why not dream big? At fifteen, she'd gone big on everything. If she swung high enough over the water to attempt three cartwheels, at least she'd get in two and one heck of a thrill before she plunged into the lake. Emily didn't have to own a cattle ranch to be happy; taking steps toward that dream would still make for a great life. She could work the James Hill Ranch full-time, even become the foreman some day. She'd know how to run a ranch, should one ever come open.

She was glad her younger self couldn't see her now. She should own at least two good working horses by now, along with all their tack, a trailer, a truck. She should've been able to afford all that because, at twenty-two, she should have been a ranch hand with four years of experience. With her riding and roping skills, she'd have been paid at the higher end of the scale for an experienced hand.

Cowboys were never rich, but she could've earned enough money for all she wanted.

Instead, she was in her fourth year of college, getting a degree only her mother wanted. Emily had so naively believed if her family knew her plans, then they'd understand why she didn't need to spend years of her life at college. Her mother, her aunt, her uncle—they'd all smiled at her with a little pity and a little kindness. *Go out and see the world, sugar. Enjoy college. There are so many options, you might find a career you'd like better.*

And then there'd been the death blow, the argument she hated the most: *Ranching is hard enough on men, sugar. I hate to see a pretty young lady choose a hard life when she hasn't even seen what else is out there.*

Not one of the smaller ranches would hire James Waterson's niece, not when it was common knowledge that her family wanted her to go to college. She'd pored over want ads in the ranching magazines, but the ranches in Montana and Wyoming that would be beyond the Waterson influence had all required four years of experience and a letter of recommendation to apply.

She'd applied anyway.

Nothing.

She'd had no choice but to go to college. Fifteen-year-old Emily would be so disappointed in her.

It's not as easy as it looks. You didn't know your whole family would be against you for trying to follow in their footsteps. I haven't given up. I'm fighting.

But it was wearing her down. Was it any wonder she'd wanted to spend one night, just this one night, with a man who took care of her? She'd just wanted to be Jane and let Tarzan keep her close to his chest, cradled in his arms. But one little taste of that, and she was hooked.

I don't want any hearts to break, he'd said.

Too late. Had he known how dangerously addictive it was for her to be around a man like him? Had he known the exact moment she'd made room for him in her dreams, had he read her mind when she'd thought that making him happy would make her happy?

I'm already half in love with you. She could have said that—but she hadn't. What had she actually said? *Let's be naked this time.*

She snort-laughed at her own words as she stepped off the rope and brushed off her hands. She'd never said anything like that before in her entire life. So much for being a shy and helpless Jane.

And yet Graham was still worried about breaking hearts. She'd given him no reason to think her heart was in danger, had she? She'd kept her feelings a secret. He couldn't be talking about her heart. And if he wasn't talking about her heart, then that left...

His.

She sneaked a peak at Graham. He was watching over her. If she somehow fell into the water right this second, he'd be there one second later, she had no doubt. He'd appointed himself her protector from the first moment at Keller's. It was crazy, the chemistry that had hit them both when they'd met. Already it was more than chemistry for her. And for him?

He'd said the only woman who mattered at all called him Graham.

She was that woman. She mattered to him. Could it be *his* heart that was in danger?

Oh, yes, please. Fall in love with me. Fall all the way.

There was nothing dangerous about loving her. He had nothing to be cautious about. She was just a college student whose dreams kept getting delayed and delayed, just a girl who...

Emily swallowed.

Just a girl who didn't stand up for herself.

She thought she was strong. She thought she was a fighter, but the truth was, her life wasn't going the way she wanted it, and year after year after year *after year*, she'd failed to be strong enough to change it. Had she been standing in the jungle all this time, passively waiting for someone to come and show her the way out?

Maybe a man like Graham knew that it was dangerous to fall in love with a woman who didn't really own her own life. He couldn't fall if he didn't think she was strong enough to catch him.

The vertigo was sudden. The rope, the dock, the wavering moonlight—the beating of her heart—scared her. She grabbed for the rope again and held on tightly to the knot, suddenly afraid to look at Graham.

Snap out of it. We don't do helpless. Get your act together.

She took a breath. She let go of the rope, turned to face Graham and started walking toward him.

"Nice dock," he said as she reached him, casual words from a man who was looking at her intently. "What do you think?"

"I think I could use that drink." She walked right past him and headed for the SUV.

The six-pack was still on the floor of the passenger seat. The locally crafted beer came in an old-fashioned bottle without a screw-off bottle cap. Her pocketknife with the bottle opener was in her purse in her truck in the parking lot. It was that kind of night.

With a sigh, she kicked her foot up behind herself and smacked the beer bottle down on it, hitting the edge of the cap on the hard wooden heel of her cowboy boot. The cap flew off and she angled the bottle away, knowing a little foam would overflow because of the impact.

A whistle of male approval sounded right behind her. "Nice technique."

"It wastes beer." She looked over her shoulder at him. *Are you falling in love with me?* "That's at least the third time tonight you've managed to get behind me without making any noise."

He reached around her to take a beer for himself. "Rubber-soled boots are quiet. They won't do me much good when it comes to opening my beer."

"Here, I can open it for you."

But Graham palmed the bottle cap and pried it off with his bare hand.

"Ouch," Emily said, trying not to be impressed by such a macho trick.

"Oo-rah," Graham said calmly.

A macho Marine trick. Even harder not to be impressed. It hit her then, that the hand that was Marine strong and apparently impervious to pain was the same hand that had touched her intimately, taken care of her—*all the way to the end*—with such gentleness, such finesse.

He tapped his bottle to hers and took a drink. She watched him, that amazing mouth, that sexy throat. *Who is this man? What is it about him that makes him a hundred times sexier than any other man?* They were the same thoughts she'd had when she'd first laid eyes on him in that dark hallway at Keller's. Never had a first impression been so accurate.

Graham gestured toward her untouched bottle. "Is nostalgia still getting to you? You quit that dock pretty suddenly."

She took a swallow. Despite the cold beer, she felt flushed. She looked away from Graham, the man who'd reined in his passion so easily, the man who was avoiding the possibility of breaking a heart, and looked toward the lake instead. The breeze was gone. The surface of the water was flawlessly calm. She wanted to churn it up, splash in it, disturb it so that it matched her emotions this night.

"It's not nostalgia." She had to answer Graham's question, when she hardly knew how to feel or what to think at the moment. "I don't belong here anymore."

He looked up from the bottle in his hand. "Did you think you would? You're on your way to getting an MBA. Profit and loss statements and power suits are a far way from a childhood pond."

"Yeah, well…" She hugged his coat around herself more tightly, when what she wanted to do was hurl her bottle into the lake to ruffle the surface. "The MBA is my mother's idea, not mine. I just found out yesterday that it's expected of me. Apparently, the details were given to Mr. Schumer before me." She sounded bitter.

She *felt* bitter. She couldn't tell Graham she was bitter that he'd chosen to keep his heart safe instead of making love to her, but she could talk about the hated MBA. "I've taken their advice and gone for a bachelor's degree. I've tried their path, but I can't keep doing this."

"Whose advice?"

"My family's. They think they're broadening my horizons. They think I'll find some new talent or a new purpose in life or I don't know what. But the truth is, I've just been a fish out of water all this time. It's been years since I felt like I lived where I belonged."

"Ah, Emily." The empathy in his voice gave her chills. "So when's the last time you felt like you belonged somewhere?"

She studied the still water. She was on the verge, on

the edge—was she daring enough to put it all together and change her life? Was she brave enough to be herself, her fifteen-year-old self, her current self, her whole self? Because that woman could be strong enough for a bodyguard who was afraid to fall.

She turned her back on the lake and faced Graham.

"I felt like I belonged tonight. In the front seat of your car."

"Ah, Emily." The bass in his voice gave her chills.

She told herself she was strong enough to ask him the same. "When's the last time you felt like you belonged somewhere, Ben Graham?"

He looked at her for another one of those long moments, the moments she realized were points of deliberation when he decided whether or not to touch her, or talk to her, or be silent and not risk breaking any hearts.

"Tonight, Emily. Tonight, in the front seat of my car."

And then she was safe in his arms, his hand pressing her head into his shoulder, her arms holding him as tightly as he was holding her.

Chapter Nine

Sex with Emily would have been less intimate than this.

They were watching the stars, sheltered from most of the cold in the back of his SUV. The hatch was up and the lights were off so they could see the night sky, but they'd shed their jackets and tucked themselves in among the new towels and the old seabags. She'd kicked off her boots so he had, too, and their feet were warm in the untried fluff of the new comforter. It wrapped around them both as Emily rested her head on his shoulder with the comforter tucked under her chin.

Graham was aware that, for a little while, his bedding would now smell like Emily. And, for the rest of his life, a deep breath of cold night air would trigger warm memories of a woman who, for one perfect night, had belonged in his arms. He might not easily remember the last woman he'd had sex with, but he'd never forget parking at a pond, fully dressed, with a Texas girl named Emily Davis.

Sex would have been easier to file away, with its beginning, middle, end. *I have to go now, good night, you're lovely, yeah, I'll see you next Saturday unless my battalion is in the field,* or once he'd begun wearing business suits instead of uniforms, *next Friday if I catch that earlier flight in from New York.*

All that wouldn't have worked with Emily—*good night, you're absolutely spectacular, I'll never see you again*—so instead he was here, baring his soul instead of his skin.

"How long were you in Afghanistan?" Emily asked.

"A year. Twice."

She paused. He breathed in the scent of her hair, tangled and windblown now, but still faintly floral. He looked at the stars.

"Were you scared?" she asked.

"Not every day."

Under the covers, she was holding his hand as it rested on his jeans, on his thigh. She gave it a squeeze. "Most days?"

"You're bored a lot of the time. You've got to stay alert while staring at the same boring landscape for days on end. As an officer, at least I could go from position to position to check on my men. But the privates and corporals were stuck at the same little piece of wall or bunker, manning the same weapon, hours or days on end. It takes mental discipline to keep your head in the game when nothing's happening for weeks at a time."

"So you had to always be on alert, waiting for something scary to happen?"

"That sounds about right."

She nodded to herself. "You still do that."

Yeah, he did. When they'd first parked here, he'd spotted the other pickup truck before it had turned on its headlights. He'd closed one eye at the first sound of an engine starting and hadn't been blinded like Emily. *Real use-ful, defending against the threat of teenagers kissing until curfew.*

Was he doing the alert thing right now? He did a mental check on himself.

No, he wasn't. He was focused on stars, on warmth, on one woman. At this moment, life was good. But she'd noticed that edgy alertness he was so tired of, and she was asking him about his combat experience. He braced himself for the mini-psychoanalysis so many civilians wanted to engage in, sharing news stories about PTSD or telling him about their friend's friend who'd been deployed.

"Did you ever have any fun?" she asked.

That wasn't the question he'd been expecting. He shifted her as she sat in his lap, so her cheek rested on his other shoulder, buying himself a little time.

It was hard to explain what passed as fun on deployment. The sense of humor was crude and macabre, but the camaraderie was real. There was no question whose back he had, or who had his back. They'd entertained themselves with tales of their families. The printed photos anyone received in a letter became nearly public property, passed around to remind each other that home existed, far away as it was. And they'd known that most of them would make it back to that home. Most of them. Almost all of them.

"We played cards. A lot. I can't tell you…" He knew his own pause was awkward as he struggled to put into words the concept of fun in a combat zone. "There isn't a dirty joke I haven't already heard twice, I can tell you that."

Under the comforter, Emily brought their joined hands up and held them against her heart. She knew. He didn't know how, but she knew that he'd given her his best answer, sorry as it was.

His heart hurt, again. Still. How much easier it would be to unzip her dress, to slip his hand under those blue ruffles and touch her soft breast instead of her soft heart.

"And then you came home and had a whole year's pay to blow on this SUV?" She had a little smile in her voice.

He rested his cheek on her hair, glad to leave Afghanistan behind. "No. I left the service. Eight years was enough. I became an executive with a civilian company that makes military gear. I made an obscene amount of money working in a much safer job. I bought this SUV because my bank balance was getting absurd."

He'd bought it because the SUV had the widest wheel base on the market, making it very unlikely to roll over. This vehicle wouldn't flip over if…wouldn't roll on him in…in a situation. He resisted the urge to rub his shoulder.

"Was this the Graham who bought cigars and golf rounds and dinners?"

"Business cards and administrative assistants. All of it."

After eight months, he'd quit. His second executive job had been with a smaller start-up enterprise. He'd thought the energy there would be different, better, but it had made him more impatient than the first—and he'd lasted half as long. He didn't belong in a suit and tie and air-conditioning, filling out reports and trying to hit sales numbers he hadn't set, no matter how obscene the money was.

"And you gave it up? Most people would be happy to have an easy job that paid well."

I didn't belong there. Graham rubbed the curve of her perfect shoulder, her body firm under the frills. He had a sudden desire not to appear like the drifter he'd become. "It was safe, not easy. It was a different kind of hard than the Marine Corps, but it was a challenge. A challenging job, money, safety. It should have been enough." He stopped himself. This was the part he couldn't figure out. Why hadn't it been enough?

It hadn't been. Something was broken or missing or worn out inside him, and he didn't know what it was. He was tired of trying to figure it out. He was going to live where it didn't matter.

"Uh-oh. You quit your job and drove from Chicago to Texas. I think I know what's coming next." She sat halfway up and twisted around to look at him, pretending to be dismayed. Since a smile was her default expression, she wasn't doing a good job of not smiling. Thank God. It gave him something to think about besides that wasted, restless year.

She not-smiled at him. "Is this the part where you tell me you're having a midlife crisis and running off to join the rodeo? You want to fulfill that boyhood dream of bucking broncos?"

"That would require me to know how to ride a horse, I assume."

She sat all the way up and faced him fully, eyes big. "You've never ridden a horse? Not once?"

"Not once."

"Never?" All the air seemed to whoosh out of her lungs, her shoulders falling. Now her smile was truly gone. "That's terrible. You've missed out on so much."

He wanted to laugh, but her pity was so sincere. *Sweet girl, that horse-crazy phase wasn't a phase for you, was it?*

"I'll teach you how," she said. "My family owns a ranch. I'll take you riding, okay? When you come back this way."

He tucked her long hair behind her ear.

"Silence isn't cool, Graham. You are coming back this way, sooner or later."

I'm leaving at dawn. But he stayed silent. She knew it already, and he didn't want to say it again.

Emily got to her knees, clutching her corner of the comforter to her neck as if she were nude and being modest as she knelt on a mattress, and holy hell, his body responded to that. *I wish you could*, she'd said. Had he really turned her down tonight? Idiot.

"When you come back, I'm going to teach you how to ride a horse. That's a promise."

He knew she sincerely thought it would be a wonderful gift to him. She was killing him with her generosity, her genuine desire to share with him what were obviously her favorite things in life. Her horses. This lake.

She sealed the promise with a kiss, kneeling over him once more, hot mouth, warm body, cold air making its way between them as the comforter was pushed aside.

My addiction, my craving...

He took her head in both hands. He kissed her harder, deeper. She trapped his hips, one knee on each side, and sank down, her dress riding up, only his denim fly and her thin underwear separating them. He gave in; he had to have her, just once, just one time. *My Emily, my heart—*

He sat back abruptly, breathing hard.

Sex with Emily *wouldn't* be less intimate than stargazing. She was such an addiction, he'd forget himself and pour everything into it. Then he'd be truly spent, with nothing left. The last piece of his soul would disappear with his heart.

He'd want to stay with his heart and soul. He'd want to stay with Emily. He couldn't. She was going back to college and a life where he couldn't belong.

Emily broke the silence. Her voice was gentle in the dark. "I only promised you a horseback ride."

"I know." He ran his thumb over her lower lip.

"It was only a kiss," she said. "I'm not pushing you to cross any line."

He paused, his thumb at the corner of her mouth.

"Graham, are you scared of me?"

He dropped his hand. He was being so easily read by a twenty-two-year-old girl with long hair and a short dress and a bright spirit. He started to shake his head like *No, I'm not scared of you*, but knew he should shake his head like *How did you know*?

Instead, he started to laugh at himself. "If I'm not, I sure as hell should be. You are something else. Come here." He pulled her off her knees to sit sideways in his lap, wrapping her in a bear hug, dropping a kiss on the side of her neck, breathing in deeply.

"So, if you don't have a secret desire to join the rodeo, where are you going? Passing through means you have a destination, right?"

The moment of light-heartedness died. She shouldn't hope. She shouldn't wait for him. He was wrong for her. He'd met her too late.

His answer was curt. "I'll be off the grid."

"That sounds mysterious. Not some undercover Marine Corps mission?"

"No."

"You wouldn't be able to tell me if it was."

He couldn't tell if she was teasing or not—but he was not. He didn't want to tell her much, but not because it was top secret. He didn't want her to hope and wait—or worse, to look for him. "No, it's nothing like that. I was offered a chance to get away from it all. A job, and I took it. I made the commitment. I need to be there in the morning."

"Yes, at dawn. I got that part. But for how long?"

He hesitated. *Don't wait for me; go live your beautiful life.* "It's open-ended."

It was an evasive answer, but it was true. Emily only had to tilt her head a single degree, only had to narrow her eyes the tiniest bit, and he knew she wasn't foolish enough to take that for an answer.

He might have been disappointed if she did.

He kissed her neck again, up high, and worked his way higher, light kisses over her jaw, a husky murmur at her ear. "I'll be working with my uncle out in the middle of nowhere. I promised him three months. Minimum."

She shivered. Poor girl, not what she wanted to hear. Then she pushed his face away. "Stop that. It tickles."

He waited.

Nothing. She'd shivered because it tickled? That was it? That was her response to *off the grid for three months or more*?

She turned so her back was to his chest, making herself comfortable by sitting between his legs, her bare legs sliding against his jeans. His arms came around her waist, of course. Prom pose, seated version.

Once again, she didn't ask him the question he was expecting. "Would you rather talk about where I'm going instead of where you're going?"

"Yes, ma'am." He'd meant to say it like a Marine, but he might have regressed to a little boy hopeful that his pretty teacher was going to tell the class a story.

Whichever it was, Emily laughed and fluffed the comforter over them. "I'll tell you where I'm supposed to go. Years ago, my mother got me to promise I'd get a college degree. I earned a degree in Farm and Ranch Management."

"I didn't know that was a major, but it sounds perfect for you."

She put her head back a little bit, talking to him almost cheek to cheek again, the way they had when they'd stood in their prom pose on the bar patio. It wasn't so innocent this time, not after she'd told him she loved his hands and the way they could please her. It would be too easy to do it again like this. He could hold her hips still between his thighs, not letting her push or press, making her wait for his hands to give her release. He'd make her wait until he'd reduced her to being only able to say *ah* and *oh* again.

"I want to go into ranching. I grew up around it. Even in San Antonio, we kept twenty head of dairy cows. I didn't want to get a college degree at all. I thought that anything I didn't already know, I could learn on the job. That's what cowboys do, but most of the college courses were actually useful. I learned some new things about soil conservation. Lots about legal requirements for livestock. Good stuff."

As he listened, Graham looked out at the stars, letting his gaze drift randomly from bright pinpoint to bright pinpoint. What a long way he'd come, from Chicago to the Marine Corps, from Asia to Afghanistan and all the way back to Chicago, before life had sent him another thousand miles southwest to Texas. It seemed like the longest journey a man could take in order to land here at the side of a pond. But here he was, content to listen to a woman who thought learning about livestock was good stuff. That same woman would willingly help him if he started to unzip her dress, yet he didn't want to stop this pleasure of hearing about an entire life spent in the hundred miles between Austin and San Antonio, with twenty cows.

"But it's an associate's degree. A two-year degree. It was cheating. I knew my mother meant the full four-year bachelor's degree when she made me promise, but I got an associate's, so technically, I'd gotten a college degree. So clever of me, right?"

He smiled as he smoothed some of her hair away from her cheek, loose tangles from the earlier breeze. "I take it you didn't get away with it."

"Not for a second."

With her hair smoothed out of the way, he put his arm under the comforter again, around her middle, ruffles tickling the inside of his wrist once more. This time, he slid his wrist up those ruffles and stopped with his arm snug under her breasts. He was aroused, anyway. He might as well torture himself for these last few hours before dawn came and he walked away.

"Cheaters never win. Since I planned my class schedule for that associate's degree, I skipped this one course in hydrology that I didn't need for the two-year degree. Now I'm getting my four-year degree in Agricultural Engineering, and guess which lousy, one-semester, three-credit course I'm missing?"

"Hydrology."

"Hydrology," she repeated, disgust in every syllable.

"Makes a good curse word, the way you say it."

She cursed again: "Hydrology."

They laughed. The sole of her bare foot pressed the top of his foot as she laughed, casually sexy, intimately friendly.

You don't walk away from this, Ben. Wake up. It's time to wake up.

He was losing his mind with these crazy-clear thoughts.

He put his other arm around Emily and laid back a little more, slouching his way down the seabags that supported his back, letting Emily lie on top of him a little more heavily. He needed her weight to keep him grounded under the infinite stars.

"I should have graduated a few weeks ago, as a December grad. I would have finished my degree in three and a half years, if it wasn't for Hydrology 201. It's ridiculous to pay for dorm and the dining hall for another entire semester—thousands of dollars—just to take this one last course, but it's a mandatory part of the degree. Here's the kicker. It's offered as an online course this coming summer. I could be done with college and start my real life now, get a real job, and just take it as a summer online course. My degree would be complete by September."

"Sounds like you have it figured out."

"My mom disagrees. Apparently, it's vital that I graduate this May and do the big cap and gown shindig. I did that for high school. I don't feel the need to do it again. Oklahoma Tech can mail me my diploma in September as far as I'm concerned, but my family just about lost their minds at that idea."

He remembered Mr. Schumer, sounding as proud as Graham imagined her family was about the MBA. "So you're going to start on your master's this semester while you finish Hydrology. Makes sense. Then you aren't spending all that dorm money on one class."

She sighed as she rested on his chest and looked out to the stars. "I'd be investing more than that. Another half a year of my life. My time. My *effort*. Once I've invested that much, I'd be expected to finish the master's, which would take both a summer session and another semester. That's more room and board, too. I'd end up spending so much more money."

She sat up, batting down the comforter impatiently so that it still covered her bare legs, but her ruffles and slender arms and long hair were free. She brooded not at the bright stars, but at the dark water. *Hydrology*.

"This is the whole reason I wanted to blow off a little steam at Keller's tonight. This is one of the things I was thinking about at the dock."

Graham sat up, too. He'd wondered why she'd come striding off that dock in such a different mood than she'd first walked out onto it.

She shifted around so she didn't have her back to him

anymore, settling in for a talk. "You're older than I am, right?"

"Mr. Schumer verified that, yeah." He winked at her, but she was too intent on her thoughts to catch it.

"So tell me what you think, since you're done with school. It goes without saying I should get that last class to finish my bachelor's, but starting a master's seems like an expensive way to do it. If I don't finish the master's, then the credits I'd earn would just be more wasted money. What would you do if you were me?"

At twenty-two, he would have stayed in Chicago and finished his MBA. He wouldn't have felt like he'd come from a different planet than the other students. Money would have been more of an issue when he was younger, though. "Who incurs the expense of another semester at the dorm? You or your family?"

"My mother assured me she could cover the cost, although I don't know where the money is supposed to come from. That makes it all the harder to say no. Who says no to a free education?"

He smiled at her, such a sweet girl. "There are worse things in the world than a family wanting to see their daughter walk across a stage and get a diploma, or wanting to help their daughter get a master's degree. You're lucky they can do it. Why not get the master's?"

She spoke gravely. "It wastes my time. I don't want it. I'll never need it."

His answer was automatic, a reflex. "You never know. Employers are looking beyond bachelor's degrees now, either in experience or education. If you have a master's—"

"No." She gripped his forearm pretty hard and stared him down harder. "I will never need an MBA. I don't want one."

In a flash, he remembered his first sight of her, being

just as firm with an ex who was treating her like she was a silly girl who didn't know her own mind: *We're through. We've been through...* Graham saw her calmly correcting Mr. Schumer: *Actually, I'm certified in first aid by Texas Rescue...*

Graham was older than Emily, but that didn't mean she was a child. If she said she'd never need an MBA, it was arrogant of him to tell her otherwise.

He nodded, just once. "Got it."

She let go of his arm. "Sorry."

"Don't apologize when you're right, especially in the business world. Especially to men." Damn, he sounded arrogant, anyway, even when he was giving good advice. But she gave him a quick nod, just once, imitating him consciously or subconsciously, before turning her attention back to the water.

She held her hands out flat, as if she could rest them on the lake surface like resting them on top of a table. "Look at how perfectly still and lovely that lake is tonight. Why make waves and ruin it? Do things the right way, the traditional way. It's safer. It's smarter. The dock should be long enough to get you out to a safe depth for diving. The rope should have knots. Be glad your family takes care of you. They only want what's best for you. There's really nothing wrong with that."

Graham watched her instead of the water or the stars.

She set her hands on her knees. "Unless, of course, that safe life is starving out the parts of yourself you liked best."

Her statement gave him pause. His dangerous life had shut down some parts of him, without a doubt, but it was the safe corporate life that had made him feel adrift. Something as safe and traditional as college could stifle someone who didn't have traditional goals. "I see why you came off that dock wanting a drink."

"It didn't seem so awful, getting that two-year degree. What's two years of your life, right? When everyone says you need a degree, it's easier to just get the degree. But then two years become four years of your life. Now five. I keep postponing my life so that everyone else will be comfortable. They don't want me to be a cowboy, so I keep not being a cowboy, year after year."

He smiled sympathetically. "I guess you'll be a very educated cowboy someday."

She didn't shy away from him, not exactly, but he could tell she was disappointed with his answer.

"Someday soon," he added, because she looked so damned sad. "Emily, you're not missing out on life. You're only twenty-two."

"What were you doing at twenty-two?"

He paused for a moment—paused and appreciated the way she was about to make her point. "I was a second lieutenant. An infantry platoon leader."

"How big is a platoon?"

"About thirty Marines. I think I see where you're going with this."

She never took her eyes off the water. "Do you? When my cousin Luke was twenty-one, he inherited one-third of a ranch. My aunt and uncle owned a third and his older brother owned a third, but they didn't want to stay on the land, so Luke ran the ranch by himself at age twenty-one. He still does. I'm twenty-two. You and Luke were living your lives when you were me. What makes everyone think I still need more schooling before I can be trusted to make my own decisions?"

She shoots; she scores.

She answered her own question. "Maybe everyone tells girls to be good and be quiet, so they don't stop and think when they're doing it to grown-up girls, too. And maybe it's my own fault. Maybe the girl doesn't notice it happening to herself, sometimes."

"Girls break that mold all the time," he reminded her gently. "Women become Marines. There must be women in ranching."

"Plenty of women run barns or teach riding, that kind of thing, but there are definite roles that are acceptable for women. I intentionally say I want to be a cowboy, not a cowgirl. Cowgirls are cute. I don't do cute very well." She glanced at him for a bare second, her smile reappearing too briefly. "The rodeo expects cowgirls to do barrel racing and only barrel racing. There's only one event where gender isn't an entry requirement. It's called team roping."

"Should I guess which event you'll enter when you have a midlife crisis and run off to join the rodeo?"

That got more of a smile, but he only got to see a piece of it while she talked to the lake instead of him. "I already compete now and then, when there's a local charity rodeo. Roping is good because either you rope that calf when he bolts out of the chute or you don't. Your horse matters a lot more than your gender. Or an MBA."

Graham didn't know what she saw in that lake, but he saw a woman who had her own opinions, her own set of values, her own way of seeing the world. She already knew how to set her personal boundaries; she wouldn't let her ex or a store owner or Graham tell her that what she knew wasn't what she knew. Now she was ready to take on the rest of the world, and she was right that an MBA would be useless in the world she was going to make for herself.

"So you're done with college," Graham said. "What's going to happen when you tell your family 'no, thanks' on the MBA?"

"If I rebel against their plans, I've been told I'll have nowhere to live. I've only got my on-campus apartment or their house. No MBA means no campus housing. As far as living with my parents, it's a big 'don't bother coming home, young lady, not when I'm willing to pay for your school.'"

Graham nodded as he rubbed his day's beard, the roughness on his palm sharpening his senses a bit. "Okay, rebel. Let's think about this. You'll need to pay for the rest of your bachelor's yourself, then. But first priority would be getting a place to live."

Finally, she was more interested in him than in the lake. That expressive face of hers looked confused. "Are you encouraging me to *not* go back to school this weekend?"

"Of course. It doesn't help any of your goals. You made perfect sense when you explained it." He angled himself to face her now that she was facing him, ready for a brainstorming session. "You need enough income to pay for the online course tuition, but not until this summer. You'll need decent internet access to take the course, but that shouldn't cost too much. How about your pickup truck? Do you have to make payments on that?"

"No, I own it." Her confusion was giving way to something that looked a little like amazement.

"So just gas money and insurance, then." He wondered why she looked so amazed. This was pretty basic brainstorming, but he explained, anyway. "If you ballpark these expenses, then you'll know what your minimum acceptable salary is when you start job interviews. It'll save you the time and effort of interviewing for positions that can't meet your needs."

"Oh, Graham." The way she breathed his name, it sounded like he'd just taken her over the edge again, given her a moment of bliss.

"What, Emily?" His voice sounded husky, even to him.

In a burst of exuberance, she closed the gap between

them, throwing herself on him, more or less, as much as the balled-up comforter that got stuck between them would allow. "Midshipman-Lieutenant-Captain-Mr. Benjamin Graham, you are wonderful."

"For laying out your expenses?" he muttered, but he had to smile at her excitement.

That quickly, she teared up. She grabbed his face in two cold hands and kissed him square on the lips, hard and fast. "You are the very first person who hasn't told me to stay where I don't want to be. I haven't had a single person agree with me and say 'go for it,' not one, not since…"

Actual tears wet her lashes as she looked up at the ceiling of the SUV, trying to recall the last time. It made Graham's heart hurt all over again.

"Not since my senior year in high school. Once it became time to apply for colleges, that was it. No one said my decision not to go to college might be valid. Not one person could accept that my associate's degree might be enough. I couldn't even get anyone to agree that taking Hydrology online this summer was the most sensible option."

She let go of his face to wipe the tears off her own. She kind of laughed and cried at the same time, reminding Graham of the soppy happy endings of the TV movies his mother watched.

"I'm sorry," Emily laugh-cried. "No, wait. I take it back. I'm not sorry. I'm not apologizing, because I haven't done anything wrong, right?"

"Oo-rah." Graham didn't know what else to say, but he could sit here until dawn and enjoy her happy face.

She wiped her cheeks. "I just didn't know how good it would feel to hear someone else talk about my goals like they should happen. I think I'll love you forever for that."

Chapter Ten

Emily could have listened to Graham brainstorm her future forever. He made it sound so normal, like she wasn't asking for a crazy dream at all.

"It boils down to pretty simple needs, a job and a place to live. What you don't need is to defer your life another semester."

I love you, I love you.

But she restrained herself and said, "Exactly, and I better find that job first thing tomorrow, or else." The image of her parents, furious at her sister, had been burned in her mind years ago. "Just...or else."

Graham looked at her intently again. She felt that sense of alertness about him, that sense that he was ready to handle danger. It had an undeniably sexy edge to it, but now that it had returned, she realized how much more relaxed he'd gotten as the night went on, here by the pond. *He smiles when he kisses me.*

He wasn't smiling now. "Your parents will kick you out? Immediately?"

"They don't believe in empty threats. I was in high school when they packed up all my sister's clothes in boxes and left them in a neat stack on the front porch for her."

"Which college didn't *she* want to go to?"

Emily kind of liked his sarcasm. "She was in the appropriate college, actually, but she got pregnant."

Graham was perfectly still for a moment. Then very deliberately, he pushed the comforter off himself and turned so he sat on the edge of the vehicle. He was tall, so his feet were on the ground as he glared at her lake. "That's a hell of a time to tell your kid she's got to find her own place to live. This is who you're dealing with?"

"They were willing to help her, but they demanded that she name the father. She refused. It was an ultimatum, tell us or else. They didn't see why the boy shouldn't have to help, or why he shouldn't face any consequences. They wanted the boy to take responsibility."

Graham's profile had that marble-statue hard look again. "I can agree with that much, but punishing the girl when she needs support is complete bull. That's not the time to throw out your own damn daughter, for fu—for God's sake."

Tarzan would be a fiercely protective father some day. It wasn't something Emily had looked for in a man before, but it was so easy at this moment to look at Graham's profile and imagine him twenty years from now. He'd be very little changed, physically. He was already a man with no trace of boyishness left. Twenty years from now, he might have some gray in his hair or some crinkles at the corners of his eyes. He'd be just as handsome, just as protective, and if he had a nineteen-year-old daughter who needed him, there'd be no conditions set first, no criteria that would entitle her to his best effort.

This night was changing her life. Graham was setting the bar so high. No wonder the plans she'd made for her future had never included a permanent relationship. She hadn't met Graham yet, so she hadn't known what was possible.

The vertigo didn't take her by surprise this time, but it was still scary, and it kept her silent.

Graham looked at her out of the corner of his eye. "Sorry. They're your parents."

"You're not supposed to apologize when you're right."

"Ah, Emily."

"Someone taught me that. Can't remember his name right now..." But Graham was still looking so deadly serious. She patted his arm, maybe a bit of a horsey pat. "It happened years ago, so it's not as shocking to me now as it is to you. But you're right about how badly my mom and stepfather handled it."

"Did they learn from it? Do you think they'd be as harsh with you over college? You're not dropping out. You're just going to get your diploma in September instead of at a ceremony in May."

"I'm afraid it'll be easier for them now that they've done it once. They are not going to have two daughters break their rules. One was unacceptable. Two will not be tolerated."

"Then you know what to expect. A predictable enemy can be planned against." He winced at his own words. "Sorry. Again. They're not your enemy. They're your parents."

"I know what you meant. My sister handled it better than they did. She's a great mom." Emily scooted over to sit next to him, her legs dangling over the edge as she nudged him, shoulder to shoulder. "She's a good sister, too. I sure learned a lesson about birth control. She made sure of that before she left. You'll notice that in the front seat tonight, at that certain moment in the dark, I said 'protection,' not 'Benjamin.'"

There was a moment of electric silence.

"They kind of sound similar. Thought maybe you hadn't caught that."

Yeah, I went there. C'mon, don't be sad on a great night.

"You are something else, Emily." Graham both laughed and gave his head a little shake of disbelief, but then he bent his head and kissed her sweetly. The comforter was now a tangled heap behind them, so Graham grabbed one of the new towels and wrapped it around her shoulders. "I'm still worried about you tomorrow. Do you have anywhere else to live?"

"Honestly, now that I've made this decision, I'm not worried at all. I'm excited, so excited. If I can't find a friend's house to crash at, I can sleep in my truck for a few days. That's the worst-case scenario."

"I don't want you to have to sleep in a truck."

"If I'm not willing to do that, then I don't want it badly enough, do I?" She looked at her lake. It was still perfectly smooth, but she was going to stir things up. A triple cartwheel, why not?

She hopped off the SUV and landed, barefoot, on the cold earth. It was shocking on the soles of her feet. It felt good. "I feel like the weight of the world is off my shoulders now, not on them. I knew the solution was so obvious. Just take one little online course over the summer, obvious, obvious, obvious. But when everyone around you thinks this big, expensive, life-changing plan is necessary, you start to wonder if you're the crazy one. I'm so glad I met you. I just needed to hear you call an online course *an online course*. That put it all in perspective. I'm not crazy. Thank you." She was keeping the towel around herself tightly, the ends in her fists, but she leaned forward and kissed Graham as sweetly as he'd kissed her. "Thank you."

"Come here." He put his hands on her hips and pulled her to stand between his knees.

Yes.

"Let's talk about timing. If you think your parents are going to kick you out in a knee-jerk reaction, can you keep your plans a secret until you find a job?"

"I'd have to find it by Sunday. That's when I'm supposed to drive back to Oklahoma." Even as she spoke, all the little pieces were falling into place. She tapped his shoulder in excitement with her fistful of towel. "Actually, the timing is perfect. I can stay at my cousin's house. It wasn't an option when I graduated from high school because my aunt and uncle lived there, and they weren't going to defy my mother. But it's been only Luke living there for years. He just got married, right before Christmas, and he's off on his honeymoon. He won't care if I crash there while he's gone."

"This is a key-under-the-doormat kind of thing? You'll be able to get in?"

"If it's even locked, yes. I was going to spend the weekend there, anyway. One last chance to ride before going back to school."

"Horses again."

"You laugh now, but you're going to love riding, too."

Graham was silent, but she let him get away with it this time. She was feeling bubbly, almost giddy with relief that she was going to stop playing by her parents' rules, but Graham was still anticipating danger for her. That sobered her up a bit.

"Instead of leaving Sunday for Oklahoma, I'll just stay on longer at Luke's." But she didn't want to sober up. She wanted Graham to smile against her lips again, so she kissed him. And she kissed him again, a little less sweetly, a little more sexily. When he took over, kissing her a little longer, tasting her a little more, she whispered, "I'll be just fine as can be."

It changed his kisses. He kissed her cheek, her temple. He smoothed her hair back and started finger-combing the worst of her tangles out. He was fussing over her. Loving her.

There was no vertigo. It didn't scare her at all to be taken care of by Graham.

"Don't spend the next three months worrying about me," she said. "I just thought of the perfect plan."

"Let's hear it."

"The timing is perfect for everything. The week before the wedding, Luke and my uncle were getting into it pretty hard in the kitchen. I told you my aunt and uncle took off once Luke turned twenty-one, right? They've been travelling all around the world, coming home only for roundup and Christmas, big events like that. Trey, the other brother, finally came home for the wedding, but it was his first time home in ten years. *Ten.* So, the gist of the conversation was that Luke is done with being left to run the whole thing three hundred and sixty-five days a year. His new wife is in charge of Texas Rescue and Relief—do you know it in Chicago? It does a lot of emergency work, natural disasters, stuff like that. Anyway, Luke's wife works in downtown Austin. They want to be able to go back and forth between the ranch house and her place downtown. I think that's fair, don't you?"

"Here, sit on my knee so your bare feet get off that cold ground."

Emily tried to play it cool when she was secretly thrilled. That gruff order meant he wanted to hear the rest of her story, and he wanted to make her more comfortable while she told it. She let him settle her on his thigh. He kept his arm around her waist.

"But my uncle, he's not going to come back to ranching. He knows ranching, he's good at it, but it's never been his passion. My mom says his father had guessed that and was afraid he'd sell the place, so the will included Luke and Trey, even though they were just itty-bitty at the time. Anyway, so there I was in the kitchen with the guys, and my uncle says to Luke that he's already put in twenty-one years, running the place until Luke could inherit it. He won't return until he's taken twenty-one years off."

"Damn. Does your whole family go so hard-core with the ultimatums?"

"Pretty much. My mother always says I'm too stubborn, but she doesn't seem to see that I come by it naturally."

"You're confident."

"I'm stubborn."

"It's attractive on you. You're going to need it to make this move."

She was reduced to that satin ribbon again, not from a sexy embrace this time, but from a compliment that made her worst trait sound like her strength. Her smile felt a little wobbly. "Have I mentioned that I'm glad you walked into my life tonight?"

Silence. The warm hand on her waist was solid, though.

"So, Luke's ultimatum was that if Trey and my uncle aren't going to help, then they're going to sink some of their share of the profits into hiring more people to work for them. For starters, they're going to hire one more hand now that the holidays are over. I could be that one. They haven't even advertised the job yet. I'm the most qualified applicant they'll ever get. Lord knows I've mucked out enough stalls in their barn for free. It won't kill them to pay me instead of hiring an outsider. I'm a shoo-in."

But the more excited she got, the more subdued Graham got.

"What do you think?" she asked.

"I think I should keep my opinions to myself," he said. "You don't need my help. I don't know how a family ranch runs, but you do. I don't know your family, but you do. I'll say this much—the only thing anyone can do is trust their own judgment and go for it. Just don't forget that there are always two possible outcomes. It will work, or it won't. You have to be ready for the 'won't.'"

"I like your opinions." He had one hand on her to keep her balanced on his knee, but his other hand was resting lightly on his other thigh. Emily gently slipped her fingers over the back of his hand and under his sleeve again, running her fingers a little way up his forearm.

"You don't think there's a chance it won't work, do you?" He turned his hand palm up. Her fingers slipped down the smooth inside of his arm. "I vaguely remember being that optimistic, back in my twenties."

"Back in your twenties? What are you now? Sixty?"

"Thirty…" His voice trailed off a little, the most unsure she'd ever heard him sound about anything.

Surely the man knew how old he was. "Thirty-what?"

"Just thirty."

She laughed a little, all part of this wonderful, bubbly, freedom-filled night. "You said 'back in your twenties' like it was eons ago. To paraphrase what some guy told me tonight, you're not missing out on life. You're only thirty."

He moved his arm so her fingers had nothing to do, but since he'd moved it in order to touch her face, knuckles smoothing over her cheek, she didn't mind.

"Eight of those years were in the Marine Corps. And

since then—" He hesitated again. "I didn't intend to meet a beautiful woman tonight and have her relying on my opinions to change her life."

"But you did, and I'm glad. Your take on the master's degree was perfect." She looped her arms around his neck, as if that would keep him close. It was an odd thing to think. It wasn't like the man was going to stand up and dump her off his lap and walk away. But he was backing out of the conversation, and she didn't want him to go.

He'd hinted at something about his time after the Marine Corps. "What were you doing in Chicago that was so awful it drove you to drive all the way to Texas?"

He was silent, but she had the feeling this was one of those deliberation points. She saw the subtle change in his expression as he made his decision and looked directly at her. Captain Graham, maybe, was going to lay it on the line. "I was getting an MBA. You are taking advice on the master's degree from a man who just dropped out of a master's degree program."

She sat back a little, she was so surprised. In the moonlight, those pasture-green eyes were almost gray, but the look in those eyes was still so direct, so unflinching, even when he was telling her something he thought was negative.

He spoke a little more softly. "I could try to make myself look better and tell you I'm taking a sabbatical."

"Don't do that. You look too good already."

His smile came and went too quickly for her to catch it with the pad of her thumb.

She traced his serious bottom lip instead, the way he had touched her mouth when she'd first told him he would be coming back to ride horses with her. "But it's not a sabbatical, is it? You don't belong there, and you're not going

back." The way he watched her lips form every word made
her feel like she was saying something erotic.

He stopped staring at her mouth. "I know what your parents would think about you going horseback riding with a
man who dropped out of his graduate school and doesn't
have a job. I'd have to agree with them."

She frowned and put her arm back around his neck.
"But you do have a job lined up. You finished your time
in the military, you worked at a safe job you hated and you
tried graduate school. That's not so awful." She wanted to
kiss him, but she kept looking in those gray-green eyes,
looking for some sign that her point was getting through
to him. "Now you're going to work with your uncle in the
middle of nowhere for three months. It sounds like you
need the break to reboot. Reset."

She couldn't stand being this close and not kissing him,
just a gentle press of her lips on his soft lips. "After that,
you're going to come and find me." Another kiss. The man
had such a hard body, a hard expression, but such soft lips.
"I'll be right here, or somewhere nearby, and I'll have the
horses ready." Another kiss.

He remained silent, but he kissed her back. Every time.

"I am going to make you feel so good, Ben Graham."

She could make him feel so good right now. She'd love
to lay him back right here in the cargo area, right here
with the old duffel bags and the new bedding. With her
hands, with her mouth, with her body, she'd make him
forget every worry. She wanted to smile over his lips the
way he'd smiled over hers, then give him one glorious moment of pure pleasure.

But he was torturing himself for some reason. He
wouldn't let her take that burden off his shoulders, not
even for a night.

Someday. Three months from now? But at this moment,

she couldn't continue to sit on a muscular thigh and be protected by a warm hand and have her every kiss returned. It made her want more. She needed to do something with all this physical passion. It was all mixed up with her exciting new plans. She was not going to waste another year of her life. Not even one semester. She was going to start living now. She was going to break that calm surface. That triple cartwheel was so close she could taste it.

A triple cartwheel. She'd never pulled one off before.

No time like the present.

"I know the perfect way to celebrate. It's kind of a bucket list thing around here that I never got to do. We should join the polar bear club. Go swimming now, while it's winter. We'll celebrate not finishing our master's degrees."

"Plunging into freezing water doesn't sound like a celebration."

"You're a big chicken if you don't do it once you're challenged."

"You're crazy, Emily Davis."

"I double-dog dare you to join me."

Silence.

"Silence is not an answer, Graham. This is an official double-dog dare to keep up with me." She pushed off his knees, backed up a step and took the towel off her shoulders. She tossed it into the SUV, then started pulling down the zipper on the side of her dress. "You're too slow. I've got less clothing to take off than you do."

She let her dress drop to the ground.

Damn him, he was doing that marble-statue thing. She'd wanted to see his eyes bug out of his head. She wasn't sure how much he could see in the dark, but her bra was pretty much just a thin bit of something see-through. He must have *felt* that there wasn't much to her bra in the front seat, but he hadn't seen it yet. In bra and panties, she turned toward the lake and started walking. Faster. A lot faster. It was cold.

He didn't exactly shout after her, but he used that Marine Corps tone on her again. "Get back in the car."

"That command didn't work last time you said it, either." She looked over her shoulder as she kept walking. "But it is sexy in an over-the-top, macho kind of way. What else you got that's over-the-top and macho?" She turned around and walked backward, keeping one arm over her breasts in that skimpy bra. "Let's see it."

"Emily, damn it."

Her bra had a front clasp. She undid it and wriggled out of one arm strap, then the other, all the while backing farther away from Graham. Keeping her arm over her breasts, she held the bra out to one side with her other hand and dropped it on the ground.

It was like dropping a start flag at a racetrack. Graham pushed off the tailgate and started heading toward her, taking long strides, kind of angry-sexy, very no-nonsense. "Emily. Enough. It's really too cold for this."

It was really was too much fun, teasing her bodyguard. She kept backing up. "I'm going in the water. If you are, too, you might want to get those jeans off. Once they're wet, they'll never dry."

Then she had to drop her arm to pull down her panties. She gave Graham less than a second to take in the full frontal view before she turned toward the lake and started running.

Chapter Eleven

That beautiful girl was insane.

It wasn't until she was nearly at the dock that Graham realized this was no game. Emily was really going in, *damn it all to hell*, and it was dangerously cold. The lake itself was dangerous. There was no way to know what lay below the surface. There was no way to know how deep the water was.

Too late, he started running after her, barefoot in the dark, pulling off his shirt and throwing it to the side.

She hit the dock running, just out of his reach. He had to stop, taking big, braking steps as he came out of a full run, cursing as he jerked his belt open and shoved his jeans and underwear off, but he was too slow, too slow.

Emily leaped for the rope at a run. She caught it high, so high that as she swung out over the water, she was far above the surface. He had only a second to pray that the water would be deep enough for her to plunge into safely from that height—and in that same second, the image of her in the moonlight was burned into his mind. She was beautiful, young and whole and all skin—*please, God, deep water*—as she let go of the rope and threw herself into a flip.

She hit the water hard. Went under.

Graham kept his eye on the entry point as he ran for the end of the dock. Just as he was throwing his arms forward to launch himself off the dock in a shallow racer's dive, Emily broke the surface with a cowboy's *yee-haw*. For a split second, his shoulder screamed with pain at being forced into the diving position, but then he dove just beneath the surface, and the shock of the cold knocked that pain out. The cold made *everything* hurt.

He surfaced quickly, right near Emily, who was still finishing the *haw* in her *yee-haw*. He shook his head once, hard, to throw some water out of his hair. A fully bellowed *oo-rah* was the only way to handle the shocking cold.

Emily laughed.

Graham used the palm of his hand to send a wave of water right at her beautiful, crazy face. As she squealed, he started to laugh, and then they were laughing together, bobbing in the freezing reflection of the moon as if they were co-conspirators in some grand joke.

For about two seconds.

"It's flipping cold," Emily said, and she started swimming for the dock.

He beat her there, but only to turn around and grab her outstretched hand and haul her in. She put her hands on the dock and kicked to get up on it, and Graham helped her with a solid hand under her bare backside. *Third time's the charm for that.*

He hauled himself out, an easy press of arm muscle that didn't bother his shoulder, which still wasn't painful because it was so damned frozen. Emily was way ahead of him, running down the dock. He walked. He thought for a second that she was yelling another *yee-haw*, but she was yelling *freez-ing*.

Hell, yeah, it's freezing. Little idiot. What did she expect? He scooped up his jeans as he stalked past them and realized he was laughing. This was insane, skinny-dipping in Texas with a woman who was old enough to know better.

Old enough. Up ahead, she bent over to scoop up her underwear. Lust hit him hard, blinding him. His navy shirt was hard enough to find in the dark without the distraction of a nude Emily as she shook dirt and leaves off a skimpy excuse for a bra.

Yet he couldn't stop smiling. The water had been so shocking, every thought had been obliterated—except Emily. *Catch Emily, be with Emily, help Emily.*

Laugh with Emily.

You don't walk away from this, Ben. You run toward it.

Acting on that crazy-clear thought, he started running after her. When Emily stopped to pick up her dress, he was close enough to see that the laughter in her face had been replaced by concentration. She was shivering to the point that she had to swipe at the dress a couple of times before she hooked it on her finger and headed for the SUV.

Just as she threw her clothes into the back, he caught up and touched her, hand on her waist, but only to push her away from the back of the SUV. "Back seat's warmer."

Water from her long hair poured over his wrist. He opened the door and chucked his jeans over to the far seat, but he didn't have to push her in this time. She climbed in fast, holding one hand below her perfect belly button, her fingers splayed to serve as a fig leaf—pretty damned effectively—and one hand trying to cover both breasts, doing a thankfully poor job of it.

It was hard not to laugh even as his teeth threatened to start chattering. He cursed loudly on general principle, because that's what anyone did in the military whenever conditions sucked, and he hustled to the back of the SUV and started pitching towels over the back seat so they landed on Emily, who'd started cursing, too.

"Holy frigging crackers, it's cold."

She had the tone of voice right. The vocabulary needed work.

He fixed it for her under his breath, shivering now as he stepped back to close the hatchback and shut out the cold for Emily, but he was still grinning at *crackers*. Emily didn't think she did cute well. She was wrong.

Then he was diving into the back seat, too, but only to haul himself halfway over the front seats to reach the ignition and start the engine. It would take a few minutes for the engine to be warm enough to turn the heater on, but at least he could get the built-in seat warmer going for Emily.

He turned around to hit the button for the rear bucket seat's warmer. Emily was staring at him so hard, he jerked to a stop. Well, damn. The interior lights had come on with their opening of the passenger door, so everything was well lit, nice and bright, as he stood completely in the buff. He'd been giving her an eyeful of his flank, his back, and now...his front. His bent thigh provided some modesty, at least. Probably. Depending her angle.

The back seat was pretty spacious, but they were still almost on top of each other because the center console made them share this half. Emily was huddled under the towels, for the most part. Glimpses of her arm and leg among the twisted towels were almost as erotic as seeing her completely nude. But it was her face, that expressive face, which arrested him. She was biting her lip in a way that might mean she was a little intimidated, maybe, but the lip she was biting curved into a smile of appreciation.

If he blushed, he'd lose his man card. Confidence, cockiness—whichever it was, he called upon it to wink at her. "Got a towel I could borrow?"

"Sure. Help yourself."

Even in a sexually charged moment, she could make him smile. He grabbed the towel from the top of the pile on her, since it wasn't actually touching her skin and wouldn't leave her exposed. She arched her back and hissed in a breath anyway, reminding him for one second of her sexual response to his touch on her breast earlier in the evening, but then she was sitting up and turning around in her seat.

"All this c-cold water keeps sliding down my back." She grabbed one of the towels and started drying the leather. "I'm just going to g-get out of your car for a moment."

"Not this time." Graham covered her hand when she grabbed the door handle. He held the bunched-up towel in his other hand and held it over his groin, in case she felt like she needed to put space between them for modesty's sake. "You're shaking with cold. I know you have a thing about getting out of my SUV, but you've got to stay and warm up."

"I have to go squeeze this water out of my hair or I'll n-never warm up."

The towels were in her lap and she clutched one to her front, but now that she was leaning forward to get out, Graham could see all that long hair plastered to her back, sopping wet. "Go ahead and do what you've got to do in here. It's only water. The carpet will dry."

"You're crazy."

"Says the woman who just went skinny-dipping in January. Come on, hurry. You're staying too cold, too long." He hit the button for the seat warmer on the other, dry seat, then twisted back to the front to reach the dashboard and start the heater.

When he turned around again, Emily was avidly watching him while she scooped all her hair to one side. He tried to get out of her way as she bent forward and started to twist it with shaking hands, wringing it out like a towel, but she raised one eyebrow and nodded toward his backside. "If I wasn't so c-cold, I'd really be enjoying this."

"You do live a wild life, sweet girl." His words were light, but the water on her exposed back was making him cold just to look at. He sat on the edge of the seat, pushing her legs over to make room, and used the towel in his hand to rub her back briskly.

"Do you have a c-comb or brush?"

"I want to get you in that dry seat first."

She gave her hair one last twist, clear water dripping onto the carpet of the floorboard and their feet. "You first. Then you can p-pull me over, like you did in the front seat."

She was too shivery, too huddled into herself to climb over that console. He rubbed her arms briskly, while she kept clutching her towel to her front. He dried himself off even more quickly. His jeans were on the dry seat, his gym bag on the floor, so he had to move them, climb over the center console without totally flashing Emily and reach over the back seats for the comforter. He reclined the seat to gain more room. If Emily were lying back, then her face wouldn't be so close to his body next time he reached for the dashboard. The footrest they'd joked about earlier came up automatically when the seat reclined.

"Do men always show off the size of their f-footrests?"

He wanted to laugh. Even frozen, she was funny to him. "Dry your feet off. Leave all that water over there."

She smacked at the water and the leaves that were stuck

to her feet with a towel. Finally, Graham sat, picked up Emily and lifted her over the center console so she was cradled in his arms again, just as she'd been in the front seat.

Hell, yeah.

There was too much skin, way too much skin, in touch with too much skin.

Complete the mission. You control your body; your body doesn't control you.

He just had to ignore her backside in his lap. Her bare backside in his bare lap. Yeah.

But that bare backside was cold to the touch. He wanted to get her skin in contact with the artificial, electric warmth of the leather seat. Concern for her made it easy to slip out from underneath her and let her lie back in the seat. He couldn't get that comforter on her fast enough, both for her warmth and his sanity, but he tried. He tucked it in tightly at her thighs, her hips, her waist. He yanked it up over her unbelievably sexy bare shoulders and tucked it in around her neck.

"There." He nodded with satisfaction at the mummy he'd created, nothing but her head showing.

"Maybe a t-towel under my head? In case my hair starts dripping? Since you have my arms trapped."

He had to climb over her a bit to grab one of the towels from the wet seat. He tucked it behind her neck, then took another towel and tried to dry her hair a bit. He kind of made a mess of it. He hoped she couldn't tell.

She wasn't even looking at his face. She was looking at his arms flex as he worked. At his shoulders. His chest, as he hovered over her. Fair enough; he'd be staring at her chest, too, if the roles were reversed. He couldn't stop smiling; she was so damned cute.

"My eyes are up here," he said drily.

"I like your tattoo."

He forgot he had it most of the time. It was a single line around one bicep. It looked like a geometric Polynesian design, narrow, only black ink. Most people never realized the design was actually made up of letters that spelled out—

"I can't read it. You have to hold still a minute."

He fell still. Most people never realized the design was actually made of words, except Emily. Of course, Emily.

"*F-I-F*...lots of *F*s. What does it say?"

"*Semper Fi*. It's the Marine Corps motto, Latin for 'Always Faithful.' And *Fortuna Fortes Juvat*." He waited until she looked from the tattoo back to his eyes. "The motto of one of the battalions I was in. 'Fortune Favors the Brave.'" It had been the battalion he'd had the company command in, deployed to Afghanistan.

Emily's lips twitched with humor, not cold. "I don't think I applied that motto correctly, then. It's what I told myself before trying to get you to kiss me on the side of the road."

This woman, she could affect him so easily. The motto had been relentlessly tied in his mind to sand, to grim victory, to sacrifice. Now he was also going to see a beautiful Texan daring to touch him, to nudge him with her shoulder, to tell him she wasn't scared of him.

He needed to put some space between them. He wrapped the damp towel around his waist as he stayed half-standing and eyed the wet chair. He could dry it off and just keep his feet off the cold puddle on the floor. The heater blew lukewarm air over his shoulders, making him shiver more than warming him.

Emily wriggled like a little caterpillar over to one side, looking so ridiculously cute again, he could shove Latin mottos to the back of his mind.

"Here, come and get next to me," she said. "The chair's getting nice and toasty now."

When he didn't move, she stopped wriggling and looked up at him. "Graham, you're cold."

"Not for long. The engine's warming up. The air will be hot in a moment. I'll sit over there."

She spoke through a clenched jaw, an angry little caterpillar. "Sit down where it's dry and don't be ridiculous."

"That schoolteacher voice isn't exactly a turn off."

"I'm not trying to turn you off or turn you on. I just want you to get your frozen butt in this toasty chair."

She was right; he'd be ridiculous to disobey her. He wasn't warming up very fast as he was. He fit himself alongside her, lying on his side to do it, so he was facing the mummy he'd made.

"All right, my butt's in the toasty chair." He was grateful for it, too.

She wriggled some of the comforter out from under herself and pulled it over his shoulders. "Here, it's mostly dry."

"You're mostly naked. Not a good idea." *Best damned idea in the world.*

"I'm all the way naked, and I'll let you know when I'm trying to turn you on. This isn't it. Besides, you're wearing a towel."

"It's a towel, not a chastity belt."

Emily kicked a little until she'd gotten some of the comforter over his feet, too. "There, now you'll warm up faster." She smiled at him once she was satisfied, a smug little grin over the comforter.

"What are you so pleased about?"

"I'd just like to point out that my schoolteacher voice works better on you than your scary military voice works on me."

He narrowed his eyes at her challenge. "I bet I can

make you take that back." *In bed, when you're begging for me again.*

She blinked, reminding him suddenly of the way she'd first looked at him back at Keller's bar. *That's right, sweet girl, you've got all my attention. All of it.*

The interior lights timed out, shutting off and leaving them in the dark. He waited in silence for their eyes to adjust, listening to the way her breath was a little shallow, a little quick, the way it had been when he'd had her body under his hands in the front seat. That little taste of his addiction hadn't been enough, not nearly enough to last him for the next three months—but it needed to be. There could be no repeat in the back seat. *If I have you once, I'll never stop craving you.* He'd tried to dismiss that thought when she'd had the steering wheel at her back, but of course, it had been true. Too true.

He needed to lighten up in the dark, for her and for himself. "If my commands don't make you stop, your own common sense should. What were we supposed to prove by taking that little swim?"

"That we're officially in the polar bear club."

He rolled his eyes and started to turn away.

She laughed in the dark. "That our parents were right and we shouldn't go swimming in January?"

"Let's go with that."

She propped herself up on one elbow, looking down at him in the gray dark. She was all smiles. He wanted her badly. He wanted to pull every last smile into himself, wanted to use her to fill up all that emptiness he'd been carrying around.

He closed his eyes against that blinding truth. Emily needed to keep running away from him if he ran toward her. She didn't need a man who needed her so badly.

"We weren't proving anything," she said, oblivious to

the serious turn of his thoughts. "We were celebrating. We're happy that I'm not going to waste another half a year of my life at Oklahoma Tech. You're happy that you aren't working at some job that pays well but sucks."

"Happy." He laid back and used one hand to rub his forehead in the sudden silence.

"Aren't you looking for happiness?" Her voice was a little more subdued.

"Happiness might be overstating it. I just crossed the border into Texas this afternoon. I wasn't coming here looking for happiness."

"What if you found it, anyway?" She rustled over him in the dark, settling her chest onto his as gently as feather down. Her skin was still cool to the touch. Her breasts, unbearably soft, gave against his hard chest. "You came here to reboot, which isn't the same as being happy. But what if, on the very first day you arrived in Texas, you found out you could be as happy as you've ever been? No broken hearts. No regrets. Could you let go of your worries and just enjoy being happy?"

Emily's question was simple on the surface. Graham lay underneath her, aware that she had depth and wisdom and a sensuality about her that went beyond bare skin and a buoyant personality.

He valued her all the more for it. Hearts and regrets and the future mattered more than ever, when they were hers.

Her hair dripped on his shoulder, as cold as ice.

"Let me get you that comb you wanted." It was a gutless change of subject, and he knew it.

He felt her cool hand as she cupped his cheek. She kissed him once, softly, a kiss as if she—as if she felt *sorry* for him. "I'll get it. Where is it?"

He raised his head, thinking to get up to get it for her, but it was a useless reflex, an automatic courtesy that served no purpose. He'd have to make her move and then he'd have to climb over her to get it. "In the gym bag. There's a shaving kit."

She plopped the bag on the center console and dug out his comb. Keeping the comforter in her teeth so it covered up her front, she pulled an already damp towel around her shoulders and then started combing her hair out, starting at the bottom, working her way up. Graham was glad the heater was blowing hot now, because the towel had to be cold as it caught more water.

He watched her in silence as she combed out her hair in the moonlight, a siren, a mermaid. He'd crossed oceans by carrier without seeing a mermaid. He'd needed to come to this little landlocked pond to find one. The thought came and went as he admired the grace in her movements, the unhurried efficiency that came from having done this same task year after year. It was such a womanly thing to comb out her long hair, as much yin to his yang as her smooth face was to his day's beard.

"You are beautiful."

She paused.

Then she took one more stroke with the comb and tossed it back in his shaving kit, tossed the wet towel onto the other seat, and tucked the comforter under her arms. Her bare shoulders were pearlescent in the gray light, her face an opal as she sat and looked out the window.

Graham ached for her, his body hard, aroused by her quiet beauty as much as he'd been aroused by more basic desires tonight.

She sighed as if she were completely satisfied. "This is the best night of my life. It already was, but it just keeps getting better. That was the most genuine compliment I've ever gotten."

"You must have had other men say you were beautiful."

She kept her eye on the stars. "Not like that."

Graham was silent.

"Do you remember when you said my prom date must be kicking himself now for passing up the chance to hold a beautiful woman?"

She asked the question as if they were having a casual conversation.

They were not.

"For the rest of your life, whenever you remember Graham and Emily by the lake that night, do you think you'll be sad that you have memories of making love to her?" She turned her gaze from the stars back to him. "Or will you only have regrets if you don't?"

Chapter Twelve

Graham and Emily, down by the lake that night.

He knew she was absolutely right. The memory of this night should be wrapped around lovemaking. The laughter and the skinny-dipping, being alone under the stars, telling their life stories, kissing, kissing—wet towels and bucket seats—everything that went with this night outdoors should be linked to deep desire, his first night in Texas, with Emily, down by the lake.

Emily brought all her hair to one side again, combed it into sections with her fingers, and started braiding it, her fingers and wrists graceful as she created one thick plait, beautiful in its tight symmetry. He hadn't known a woman braiding her hair would sharpen his craving to this point. The comforter she'd tucked under her arms was secure on one side, but her other arm had to reach farther to work on the braid, and the comforter slipped a little lower. And lower, exposing a perfect curve, still hiding the perfect nipple he'd seen at the dock, in the dark.

"By the way," Emily said, her smile coy once more, "this is the part where I try to turn you on."

"Done." His heart hurt. His body hurt. He didn't know how he was going to keep breathing, but he managed that one word.

"I saw this when I got the comb." Done with her braid, Emily reached into his shaving kit and pulled out, very delicately between finger and thumb, one shiny foil packet.

Thank God he had a condom.

She lifted her hand higher. A second packet was attached to the first. Then a third packet. Emily's laughter filled the back seat as she whipped out the rest of the strip.

Thank God for the laughter, too. Graham couldn't take much more raw emotion, not after the years he'd spent feeling empty.

"You said I'd be a nymphomaniac if I pulled a whole strip of condoms out of my cowboy boot." She was all smiles, the strip dangling from her fingers. "What does this make you?"

"A happy man." He grabbed the strip from her and tore the first one open with his teeth.

She knelt over him once more, a knee on either side of his hips. He shoved aside the towel, the comforter, and they were bared to each other completely, that quickly. His senses were overwhelmed. He couldn't look enough at her, couldn't feel enough of her as her body touched his in a dozen places at once, her fingers curved around his bicep like a tattoo, her toes tucked under his knee. He could barely take his eyes off her long enough to turn his head and spit out the torn foil as he tossed the rest of the strip aside. He sheathed himself with a trembling hand.

"This is going to be so fun," Emily said in a purr that was far cuter than she knew. "We're naked this time."

"Hell, yeah."

But bucket seats had their limitations. He had to give her quiet directions, *let me slide down a bit, you slide up, keep your knee there, sweet girl*. He kept a hand on her lower back, guided himself into position, pressed her down as he thrust upward—and nearly died from the perfection.

There was nothing light about it, nothing cute or funny, just intense pleasure. The sound he made deep in his throat was one of surrender to the hit of pleasure. He couldn't stand the pleasure, not when he was trained only to withstand pain.

He needed to finish this before it finished him, a desperate man who was desperate to end the pleasure. Emily—Emily, perfect Emily—moved with him, helped him, cried out with him as they brought the pleasure directly to its crashing, crushing finish.

Graham held Emily tightly to his chest.

He couldn't speak. He'd never be able to explain how hard it was to have his body, heart and soul all register bliss instead of agony. It was certain bliss to be with the right person in the right place. He needed to make this work between them. He'd find a way to make their lives mesh. But God, he couldn't speak right now. He felt too close to crying.

Emily regained her breath first. Her hand grew steadier as she smoothed his hair back. When she lifted herself a little way off his chest, he had to close his eyes.

"Graham…"

Don't tell me how you feel, don't ask me how I feel, I can't talk, I can't cry…

"Graham, how many condoms are left?"

It wasn't the question he was expecting. He was so grateful it wasn't the question he was expecting. He managed to let go of her with one arm to pat around the edge of the seat until he found the strip. He held it up and opened one eye to squint at it over Emily's shoulder and her thick braid. "Five."

"In that case," she said, pushing herself up far enough to look into his vulnerable face, "I'm not nearly done welcoming you to the great state of Texas."

And Graham found that he didn't need to cry. He could laugh.

It would be dawn soon. The world was becoming a lighter shade of gray. The first color would appear, and he would have to disappear from Emily's life. For a while. For too long.

She slept on his chest, tired out from happiness.

It felt so serious. It all felt so damned serious.

Wake up, Ben.

He was awake now. It only amazed him how long he'd been in a fog. Before grad school, before the corporate jobs, he'd been losing himself, fading away during the last year in the Marines. He'd been wasting time, wasting money. That one semester of grad school had sucked fifty thousand straight out of his bank account, the price of an elite institution. He still had some money, but he couldn't keep this up, drifting from job to school to job, not if he wanted to be a permanent part of Emily's life.

That was exactly what he wanted to be.

He'd come to Texas hoping the empty space would match his empty soul, but now he needed those three months to get his act together—to reboot, to reset, just as Emily had said. If he'd thought earlier tonight that he'd met her too late, he'd been wrong. He'd met her too soon. Three months too soon.

He needed that reboot, and he knew it. He'd also known that if he had Emily once, he'd be craving her forever. Well, he'd had her. Now he'd pay that price and miss her every day. He kissed her as she slept. He kissed her while he still could.

It had been worth it.

She had her own life to square away. Would she be missing him as much as he'd be missing her? He hoped to hell she would, so she'd be waiting for him. He hoped to hell she wouldn't, because he didn't want her to be in pain, not the girl with the easy smile.

These were his thoughts as dawn approached. With the light, color returned. He watched her hair turn from charcoal to warm brown, her white shoulder turn to pale gold. He woke her, so as her ruffled dress turned blue, she could put it on. Then they drove back to her truck, parked by the bar that stood all alone on the side of the road.

She seemed more delicate in the dawn. During the night, she'd taken the lead. He'd been at her mercy, unable to do anything but accept the smiles she gave him, to laugh when she made him laugh, to feel all the pleasure she poured into him, even when it overwhelmed him. But now, with gravel crunching under their boots as they walked from his vehicle to hers, Graham felt all her vulnerability. Defying her parents was going to take a toll on her. Graham knew it, even if she did not. In the end, he hoped it paid off. Either it would work, or it wouldn't.

She hadn't made a plan for the *wouldn't*. He wasn't going to be around to help. *Three months too soon.*

His Marine Corps jacket was too big for her, making her seem as fragile as she'd claimed she wouldn't be if they had sex before he drove away at dawn. His first instinct had been right; he couldn't be her lover and leave, and he couldn't be her lover and stay. The better word would have been *shouldn't*. He shouldn't have been her lover, but he had been, and there was no going back on that now.

She barely let any sadness show through her smile as

she gestured to her truck. "My jacket's in there. No problem, so here's yours." She started to unzip his jacket.

"Keep it."

"I can't. Everyone will wonder who gave me a Marine uniform. The inquisition will begin immediately."

"Lie and tell them you bought it at an Army-Navy store in Austin."

She hesitated.

He zipped the jacket up halfway. "It'll keep them guessing next time you go to Keller's. They might behave if they think a Marine is about to come out of that bathroom looking for you. Or maybe they'll think you're the Marine."

Her smile was directed at the gravel. "I'll really be okay. I can handle myself and most anyone else, when there's no handsome man around to swoop in and save me." She kicked a rock with the toe of her boot, then she stuffed her hands in the pockets of his jacket and lifted her chin. "Well, I guess this is it. That sun is coming up. You don't want to be late—"

Graham pulled her close and gave her mouth something better to do than tell him goodbye.

She melted into him like she was a part of him, as she'd been so many times in the dark. By the time they stopped kissing, he had her up against the truck. She had him up against her body, pulling him closer with one hand under his shirt, warm on his skin, and one tucked under his waistband, as if her hand was the back pocket of his Levi's. They spoke against each other's lips at the same time.

"If your parents come to get you at your cousin's house—"

"I know you have to go—"

They both fell silent.

Emily slipped her hands out from under his clothes, letting him go. "Don't worry about me. Go and lose yourself in your work, or find yourself. This isn't goodbye forever. You're going to remember this night, and you're going to want to see me again." She kissed him then, a sexy taste of her tongue, an unmistakable invitation to take her to bed. "You're coming back for more of this."

"You're right."

She sucked in a little breath, sharp and short, like his words were a needle that had pricked her finger. "Say that again."

"You're right, Emily. I'm coming back for you."

"Oh—that's such a better answer than silence." Her tears caught them both by surprise.

Graham tucked her head onto his shoulder. "You've been telling me all night I was going to come and find you when my contract was up. You sure sounded certain. Did you doubt it?"

"No, I know I'll see you again. It would kill you to spend the rest of your life wondering what might have been. But you were pretty stubborn about admitting you even wanted to kiss me at first. Who knows how long you could be stubborn about more? I could imagine you wasting at least a year, telling yourself you were too old for me or those eight years in the Marines were too much for me to handle. I was afraid you'd wait until the 'might have been' was killing you."

"I'd be insulted if that wasn't so damned accurate." He breathed her in, then let her go.

"We value our accuracy, don't we?"

"Ah, Emily. The day my contract is up, I'm coming for you."

She leaned back against her truck and tugged him toward her, fingers hooked in his belt loops like she owned him. "One more minute. The sun hasn't cracked that horizon yet. Where exactly are you going to be? Where is off the grid?"

"Not this county. Not the next, either. I have to find it by GPS. There aren't any buildings or crossroads nearby, but my uncle called me yesterday morning, so he must get a cell phone signal now and then. I won't be totally out of touch. You have my number. I have yours. I'll find you."

She'd pulled him to her so he was pressing her into the side of the truck as if he were pressing her into a mattress. He leaned in a little harder, pinning her in place so she'd listen to him, this woman he'd met before he was ready.

Not ready? Too bad. Adjust fire, Marine.

"I'm not going to bother with the scary military voice, but listen this time. If your plan goes sour, you call me. If I don't answer, leave a message, because I'll be doing everything I can to get a signal as often as I can. I don't want you sleeping in your truck tonight."

"What are you going to do at the end of your first day on your new job? Come driving all the way back here from two counties over? You can't go another twenty-four hours without sleep."

"Yes, I can. I've done it for worse reasons. You call me when you need me."

As he was looking at her, the first rays of the sun touched her face. The world was coming into vivid, full color. He had to let her go.

"I'm worried about you." He kissed her forehead tenderly, a benediction. "Stay safe, Emily Davis."

"It's Dawn."

"I know."

"I mean my middle name is Dawn. If you're going to get all paternal on me, then you might as well use my whole name. Go all out." She imitated his gruff voice. "Emily

Dawn Davis, you be a good little girl now. Play nice with the other kids."

He took a step back.

"Seriously, do you realize you just kissed me on the forehead? You should be giving me a 'yee-haw' or an 'oo-rah' or something. Today is the day. I'm off to do my own thing and listen to my own instincts. I'm stirring things up and living life, and you should be saying 'Go kick some ass, girlfriend.'"

For one speechless second, Graham stared at her. Then he looked up at the colorful sky and started to laugh. Man, he was in love. There was no way not to be.

"All right, Emily Dawn Davis." He grabbed her in a bear hug and spun her around once in the gravel parking lot for good measure. "Give 'em hell."

He set her down and opened her door, but before she could sit, he smacked her on one butt cheek, hard.

She yipped. "What was that for?"

"That's how an Airborne School jumpmaster tells you and your parachute it's time to get the hell out of his nice, safe airplane."

"They spank soldiers on the butt?"

"It's an Army school. You can't expect advanced communication. Now go jump out of your nice, safe plane. Before you hit the ground running, don't forget to look at the horizon and enjoy the view."

Chapter Thirteen

Emily had no reason to be sad.

She was driving toward her favorite place in the world, the James Hill Ranch, after having the best night of her life. She'd gone into that night with her eyes wide open. She'd known she'd be alone today.

I'm coming back for you. Her tears at those words had taken her by surprise. She'd already known he'd be back, someday. She really had. Still, hearing him say it this morning had touched something inside her, something that made her want to cry.

But she was fine now.

Schumer's convenience store was up ahead, on the right. Emily craved some caffeine, but stopping in for a cup while she wore the same dress she'd had on before midnight? That was not going to happen, no matter how badly she needed coffee. Mr. Schumer might expire of excitement as he jumped to all the right conclusions. Yup, she and Chicago had indeed had sex, just as he'd predicted.

Hours of it. Great sex—it had been the best sex of her life. At thirty, Graham was the oldest man she'd ever dated, with a man's body and a man's experience. He knew what he was doing. But when she was with him, so did she. Her touches, her kisses, the way she moved, the way she sighed, everything she did had pleased Graham. He'd told her, he'd shown her, he'd wanted her over and over. She could do no wrong. *Addicted,* he'd murmured more than once.

Her throat felt tight, her eyes burned. These memories ought to make her feel confident, not make her cry.

She wanted to go back and drive real slow past the spot where they'd first kissed. She'd remember how confident she'd been then, making the first move for that first kiss. Then she could keep driving, all the way back to Austin, and put her confidence to use. The first step really ought to be sitting down with her mother and stepfather and talking about that master's degree. But her mom thought she'd spent the night at her aunt and uncle's house at the ranch. Mom would be shocked if Emily walked in the door with a wet braid and a party dress on. It would be tough to steer the conversation toward MBAs and bachelor's degrees.

Emily tightened her grip on her steering wheel. She was twenty-two and ready to move out and start her own life, her own career. She shouldn't have to answer to anyone about wet hair and party dresses—but she wasn't there yet.

She would be. But this morning, maybe she should start at the James Hill, get everything lined up there, and then tackle that conversation with her mother later—like on Sunday, when she wouldn't be driving back to Oklahoma, after all.

The gate for the James Hill Ranch, like most ranch

gates in Texas, was simply made out of two tall poles and a crossbeam. The brand for the ranch was a straightforward JHR, so those initials marked the entrance. Her truck rattled pleasantly over a cattle guard—it was a sound she missed all semester, every semester—and then she drove through the more formal wrought iron and limestone pillars of the second gate. There, spread before her across a bit of a rise—the hill in the James Hill—were the main buildings of the ranch. Three barns, the cow sheds, the garages, the bunkhouse.

After she was officially hired, she'd start living in the bunkhouse. Cowboys got lodging there as part of their compensation, and she was going to need that, a private bedroom and a shared kitchen, because her mother and stepfather were not going to be speaking to her for a while. Instead of making her feel angry, the reality of their ultimatums made her sad.

The road curved a little to the left, and the main house was straight ahead. A sense of homesickness blended with gratitude that it was still there, her aunt and uncle's house, her vacation paradise as a child, her sanctuary as a teenager. Her aunt and uncle were traveling to the bottom of the globe to see penguins or something right now. Trey lived out of state and had for a decade. Luke was on his honeymoon, but the house was here, the one house that had stayed constant for twenty-two years.

She needed it now—but not to spend the night. She'd settle the job this morning and move into the bunkhouse tonight. She was looking forward to that, a real place of her own where real adults lived instead of student housing, but she could hardly go and talk to the foreman about the job while she was in last night's mini dress. She needed to go into the house and get showered and get some working clothes on.

She parked around the back, next to a shiny new hybrid sedan. Maybe it belonged to Luke's new wife, although he'd married into an oil baron's family, and Emily couldn't imagine his elegant bride driving such a practical little vehicle.

Emily tried the door to the mudroom. It was unlocked, but that wasn't unusual. She used the boot jack to take off her fancy boots, then she dropped her real boots, her working cowboy boots, by the door as well, so she could put them on as she was leaving the house for the barn.

It wasn't until she saw the cereal bowl and coffee cup in the kitchen sink that she realized someone else was living in the house. "Hello? Anybody home?"

She hoped not. She didn't feel like being sociable after her night with Graham. She just needed to take a shower and change into work clothes, then go to the foreman's office and tell Gus she was ready to take the position—

A woman her own age walked briskly into the black-and-white kitchen and came to a sudden stop. "Emily? You're back."

"Rebecca? You're still here?" *Oh, my gosh. What a rude thing to say.* "Wait, let me try that again. Rebecca, you're still here. It's nice to see you again."

Rebecca smiled, still as sweet as Emily remembered from Luke's wedding. She was the sister of the bride, which made her Luke's new sister-in-law. Emily supposed it wasn't that unusual for Luke's sister-in-law to be at his house, except for the fact that Rebecca lived in Massachusetts and the wedding had been weeks ago, before Christmas. She must have decided to extend her visit to Texas instead of returning right away to snowy Boston.

Yes, Rebecca was perfectly sweet and friendly—so Emily hoped she'd forgive her bad manners now. Emily just couldn't keep up a normal conversation. She just couldn't. She'd been banking on the house being empty.

Emily had a death grip on the jeans and fresh clothes she was carrying. "Are you using Trey's bedroom?"

Rebecca seemed startled by that question. "Um—"

"I mean the guest bedroom with the big trophy shelf. That used to be Trey's room." Emily held up the clothes. "I was just going to dump these there and take a quick shower and change before I go to the barn, because I'm, uh, not dressed for the barn. Not really."

Not even close. Please don't ask me why I'm standing here barefoot in a mini dress with a wet braid, wearing a Marine Corps track jacket. She was blanking out on a reason she might be dressed like this, besides *I met a man at a bar, and we went skinny-dipping in Cooper's pond and had sex until we were worn out, and I guess this jacket is kind of a souvenir,* which made something really wonderful sound really, really terrible. Emily inched her way toward the doorway to the rest of the house, longing for escape.

Rebecca kind of inched her way toward the mudroom door. "I'm so happy to see you again, and I really want to catch up, but I have to go to a job interview in Austin."

"You're moving to Texas? That's great. Really great." *I can't do this, I can't make small talk when I can still taste Graham on my lips.* She missed him. She wanted to be with him right now.

Rebecca and Emily continued circling each other gingerly as they talked, until Rebecca was closest to the mudroom and Emily was ready to bolt into the living room.

"We'll catch up later, then? I've got to…" Rebecca looked at the wall clock apologetically.

"Yes. Good luck." And then Rebecca was out the door and Emily was all but running through the house to Trey's old room. She dumped the fresh clothes on the bed and backed far away from them. They smelled like fresh laundry, and holding them was making her arm smell like fresh laundry. She wanted to smell like a fresh lake and moonlight and Graham's warm skin.

She walked into the bathroom, took one look at the shower stall and started to cry. She didn't want to jump out of that airplane and jump into the shower. Her skin smelled like Graham's skin, and she didn't want to lose that. Not yet.

But she was going to lose it. She'd done such a good job acting confident, telling Graham not to worry about her, telling him not to act like he was her parent. She didn't want to be a burden he'd carry for three months, and she'd made sure his last impression of her was a fearless woman who was going to be so busy, he might as well take his whole three months to work with his uncle and focus on whatever issues had driven him from Chicago to a new life.

She'd pulled the charade off and left him laughing. The only reason she'd been able to pull it off was because she loved Graham.

Otherwise, she would have crumpled like that ribbon at his feet and begged him to stay. She was just a fragile girl, she'd wanted to say. He couldn't dump Jane back in the jungle without him; she had no defenses. He needed to hold her for hours and reassure her that he'd never leave her.

But he might leave her. He'd acknowledged the truth behind her theory that he might talk himself into believing she was better off without him. He'd called her an addiction. Didn't men try to break addictions?

What if she never, ever smelled like Graham again?

Emily left the bathroom. She just needed a little longer, just a little longer, to remember the taste and feel of Ben Graham before she washed it all away.

She curled up on the bed and cried herself to sleep, wrapped in an olive drab track jacket.

The best night of his life was being followed by the worst morning of his life.

No, he couldn't say that. The morning his convoy had been hit had been the worst morning. Men had died. Good men.

Graham wanted to punch something. One of the frustrating things about being a combat veteran was that he couldn't ever complain that any day, no matter how awful, was really the worst day. Watching Emily Davis drive away from a bar's empty parking lot—blowing him a kiss and smiling at him—tore his heart out, but nobody was literally dead. The standard had been set as low as it could get: no day could be the worst if there were no corpses lying around. Combat had stolen his ability to complain.

He hit the steering wheel. Screw Afghanistan. It wasn't going to deny him the right to say this morning was painful. He missed Emily the way he'd miss a part of his body—something essential, like his heart. He'd known there was something special about *Em* from the first minute. He'd *known* he was risking what heart he had left when he'd held her on that bar patio. Knowing heartbreak was coming didn't make it less painful when it came.

And now he was lost. Lost and late.

If there was one thing a Marine was not, it was late. To be fifteen minutes early was on time. To be on time was to be late. To be late was to be dead.

More death.

Sunrise was long past. The sun was up and there was no cattle ranch in sight.

He'd driven sixty miles from Keller's, so far. He wouldn't cause more gossip by using Schumer's restroom to shave and make himself presentable for his uncle, but thirty miles had passed as he'd headed toward his uncle's ranch before Graham saw another gas station. He'd stopped there and done his best in a cold-water sink. At least the coffee they sold was hot.

He'd driven another thirty miles since then. Now the blue dot on his phone's GPS map said he should be looking at the James Hill Ranch. He was looking at nothing, just endless terrain sparsely covered with shrubs, all of it brown in January. A plateau in the distance was so abruptly flat that it looked like someone had sliced the pointed peak off a mountain.

He would've thought he'd found some virgin wilderness untouched by civilization were it not for the presence of a fence along the edge of the road, miles and miles of single-strand barbed wire nailed to wooden posts. It wasn't the kind of concertina wire they used in the military. This fence wasn't made to hurt men, just to set a boundary.

He had a signal for his cell phone, so he pulled off the road, stopping on the shoulder. *Emily kissed me on the shoulder of this road, sixty miles back.*

Yeah, well, nothing that great was going to happen to him again, not for another three months, at least. He needed to get used to that hollow feeling in his chest.

He called his uncle, told him which county he was in and the number from the last mile marker sign.

"I was afraid you'd changed your mind, son. Glad to hear from you. You're just a little too far west. Head back toward town." Uncle Gus always spoke slowly, like he had all the time in the world.

"I'll be there as soon as possible. It won't happen again." Had this been his first day in the Marine Corps, Graham would've been lucky to get away with dropping for push-ups in a sawdust pit until his arms could no longer support his own weight and he smashed his sweating face into the sawdust.

Uncle Gus didn't sound like being two hours later than expected was much of a problem. "That GPS took you to the James Hill. It just took you to the far hundred. My guess is you're looking at the western property line. You need to head east about fifty miles to get to the ranch buildings."

The ranch was fifty miles wide? How many millions of dollars did fifty miles of land cost? Graham thought of Emily and her twenty dairy cows. Her family ranch sounded like a cozy world, far different from this commercial cattle operation.

"The gate is marked with a JHR. North side of the road. If you hit a gas station called Schumer's, you've gone too far. Just drive up to the ranch buildings. My office is in the third barn to the east."

Schumer's? *Schumer's?*

Graham hung up and did a U-turn, heading in the right direction. His morning still sucked, but it wasn't the worst ever, and not just because there was no body count. He was wasting time and gas on a hundred-and-twenty-mile, completely unnecessary round trip to nowhere, but that trip was going to land him somewhere in the vicinity of Emily's family ranch.

Uncle Gus would know of the Davis place, surely. If Emily's cousin's name wasn't Davis, Graham had no doubt Mr. Schumer could tell him where a local man named Luke owned a ranch. One thing was for certain: Graham was going to be able to see Emily. Soon. Often—as long as her cousin gave her the job this morning.

He drove a little faster, an addict craving one more hit. Graham hoped ol' Cousin Luke wouldn't put Emily through a wringer. She was going to have a tough enough time with her mother. *Just give her the job. She'll be so happy.*

And she'd be here, in the middle of nowhere with him, instead of at Oklahoma Tech University.

The middle of nowhere might be just where he belonged.

Chapter Fourteen

Graham's first sight of the James Hill Ranch was an eye-opener.

It looked like a small town itself, maybe a dozen buildings. What it did not look like was the middle of nowhere. All of Graham's expectations evaporated like a puff of morning mist. Where had he gotten the idea that Uncle Gus lived in some kind of remote hunting and fishing cabin?

Gus met him as Graham got out of his SUV. Gus Montano looked older than Graham remembered, but he moved like a man in good physical condition. Maybe *weathered* was a better description than *old*. His uncle was weathered, a stereotypical cowboy. Uncle Gus wore a cowboy hat and spoke with a Texas drawl. When he was a very young man, he'd left Illinois for a two-year stint in the army and had never returned, except for Christmas every even-numbered year. He'd lived in Texas for at least forty years now, so that accent sounded as authentic as his hat looked.

Graham shook hands and thanked him for the job. Gus got misty-eyed and pulled him into a hug and told him how much he looked like his mama, Gus's little baby sister. *You've got the Montano look, boy, always did.* A hug— when was the last time Graham had been hugged by another man? It was disconcerting, being treated like some kind of prodigal son. Graham had to readjust his thinking yet again. He wasn't being treated like a shiftless drifter who was getting bailed out by a blood relative. Gus was genuinely excited to have him working here.

Being men, Gus and Graham soon turned to talking about Graham's vehicle. "I've heard about these," Gus said, opening doors and checking it out.

Graham stood steady, a good Marine, when he wanted to jump out of his skin as he watched his uncle unknowingly erasing traces of Emily. Gus opened doors, thumped the seats and ran his hand over the center console, and Graham tried not to feel the loss of the last of the floral shampoo and vanilla lip gloss that he'd spent a hundred and twenty miles believing still clung to the leather.

"You've got a real nice ride here," Gus said approvingly.

He sounded like Emily; it must be a local thing, that *real nice ride.* Graham gave his uncle the keys and let him drive the SUV to the bunkhouse, Graham's new home.

"You're sure you don't want to stay in my house, now? The offer stands. Plenty of room to put a roll-away in the living room."

That was where Graham had gotten the idea that his uncle lived in a small cabin. "I'm sure, but thank you." He slung one seabag over his good shoulder and carried the other in his hand.

His uncle grabbed a towel. It was still soaking wet. It was amazing, really, how much water Emily's hair had held. Her braid hadn't dried much at all by morning.

Gus said nothing, until he grabbed a second towel. The tags were still on the third one. "What the—where do you buy wet towels?" Since Gus was chuckling, Graham chuckled, too. *Don't ask me anything.*

It didn't deter his uncle. He picked up the last towel and made a show of looking at the cargo area's light. "This vehicle has a shower in it, too?"

What excuse was there to have wet towels? Graham fell back on the facts. "Nah, I went swimming."

"In January?"

He had a reputation to protect: Emily's. Word got around in a small town. He wasn't going to confess to any pond's polar bear club. He hated to lie, but it was for a good cause. The best cause. Her cause. "The hotel had a heated swimming pool."

Gus piled all the towels into one arm and grabbed the comforter. Graham heard Emily's voice as she'd wriggled out of her mummy wrap to include him. *It's mostly dry.*

Gus led the way toward the bunkhouse, shaking his head. "I guess youth isn't wasted on the young. Someone at your hotel left a few strands of long hair on this here wet comforter. Hope you didn't leave any broken hearts in the city."

"Only my own."

His uncle scrutinized him from under the brim of his cowboy hat.

"Just kidding. Really."

Not kidding. My heart's gone.

The girl who had taken it had left long hair on his comforter, and his uncle had too damned sharp of an eye. Now if Graham asked his uncle if he knew a local girl named Emily Davis, it'd be too revealing. Damn, damn, damn. He was going to have to wait for the right time to drop her name.

He followed his uncle into the bunkhouse. It was a distinctly male space. Graham scanned left to right. Checked the corners. *Clear.*

A billiards table, overstuffed armchairs grouped a little haphazardly around a TV, and a basic kitchen made up the common area. His bedroom was private and simple, an extra-long twin bed and a desk, the only unoccupied room in a hallway of six identical rooms. It reminded him of barracks. Three months of solitude would never be found in barracks.

Graham looked at the bed and knew he'd never bring Emily here. He'd have to find a hotel on the edge of Austin that really did have a heated swimming pool.

"You can unpack later, son. Let's go get your signature on this contract. Now, I usually sign 'em, being the foreman, but since you're my nephew, it'll be better if one of the owners signs. The only owner on the property right now is Trey Waterson. I'll introduce you."

"Trey. Do I know that name?" He followed Gus on foot back toward the barns. No wonder the older man seemed to be in good shape. Just going from building to building around here was going to add miles of walking to Graham's day. He'd need no more gym workouts to offset air-conditioned days of immobility spent tied to a desk.

"His name was out there, a while back," Gus said. "Trey was a big football star in his college days. Oklahoma Tech. Quarterback. Heisman candidate his freshman year."

"No sh—no kidding? That's got to be it." Except something about the name had made Graham think of Emily, not football. The Oklahoma Tech connection made him think of Emily, maybe. Or maybe it was because Emily was pretty much all he could think about. He needed to focus on the here and now to meet his new boss, who was outside near a split rail fence.

Trey Waterson had all the size of an NFL star. Graham didn't normally look up when he talked to another man. That was a novelty. They were probably the same age, but Trey owned the place, and Graham had no problem with rank structure after eight years in the Marines, so when Gus walked him over to introduce him, Graham shook hands and said, "Mr. Waterson."

"Call me Trey. You go by Benjamin?"

"Graham."

"All right, then. Gus tells me you're a veteran. Thank you for your service."

Graham didn't know how to respond when people said that. *Sure, you're welcome for me being the one in the vehicle that flipped when that roadside bomb detonated. The shoulder sucks, but other Marines got it worse, so I can't complain.*

Graham nodded and hoped that would suffice. He knew people meant well when they thanked him, but it was the kind of thing he'd hoped to avoid out in the middle of nowhere. He'd left Chicago expressly so he wouldn't have to pretend like he was sociable in any kind of group, yet here he was, forced to deal with the polite conventions of society even on a cattle ranch.

The two men seemed to think a nod was plenty. No further questions or comments. That was good.

They started walking toward one of the barns. Graham fell into step with them. It was a little bit like walking with John Wayne or Clint Eastwood, the stereotype was that realistic. Since Graham didn't know anything about the real West, he watched Gus and Trey. They did the same kind of alert scan that had become second nature to Graham in the military, only these men were looking at the buildings in general, maybe the sky at the horizon, too, and checking out the horses in a pasture in particular.

Horses. Graham hadn't expected there to be so many, a couple dozen of them, grazing on the other side of that split rail fence. They were impressive in their size this close. Their musculature under their brown and black coats looked as sleek as any horse he'd ever seen on television or a racetrack, but this close, he could appreciate the power these animals must be able to produce when they worked. They weren't working now. They swished their tails or took a few steps as they nosed around the ground, but mostly, they just looked peaceful. Patient.

Ah, Emily. This was the type of place where she felt like she belonged. Here, and in the front seat of his SUV. The back seat. *My arms. She belongs in my arms.*

"You ride?"

Trey's voice jarred his attention away from the horses. "Haven't tried it."

"Gus did say that, now that you mention it." Trey shook his head a little, like it was incredible a grown man hadn't saddled up a horse in his life. Same attitude as Emily, male version. "You know cattle?"

"Never touched a cow."

Trey seemed amused by that one. "If you make it to roundup, you're gonna touch a thousand of 'em and probably wish you hadn't."

Trey eyed him another moment as they walked. Graham returned the look with a level gaze. He didn't know squat about ranching, but if the military had taught him anything, it was that a person could do just about anything they had to do when they really had to do it. Vault fences, jump out of planes, go days without sleep, apply a tourniquet and drag an unconscious buddy half a mile in hundred-degree heat until the helicopters came. Whatever one had to do.

They walked into one of the barns. *Left to right, check*

the corners. This place would be a nightmare to clear of enemy personnel. Every stall could hide ten men.

Gus's office was a walled-in space off to the right. The contract was waiting on his desk.

"You know how to change motor oil?" Trey asked, taking off one of the leather work gloves he wore.

"Yes." *Finally, a yes.*

Trey signed his name on the contract, tossed down the pen and put on the glove again. "We've got two ATVs due for oil changes. Since you'll be riding those while you learn which end of a horse means business, you might do the changing yourself. We keep 'em in the shed that's closest to the house."

Graham signed his name on the dotted line.

"After that," Trey said with an actual smile, "you gotta shovel some manure."

Graham settled for a nod. After all, he was the one who'd be doing the actual shoveling. "Understood. That's the way most jobs go."

"Welcome aboard." Trey smacked him on the shoulder. Luckily, on the good shoulder, because the man did not play. If Graham hadn't been a Marine, he had no doubt these cowboys would have him facedown in the dust. Graham swallowed his *oof* and did not stumble forward from the impact. *Semper fi, gentlemen.*

Trey turned to leave. "Gus, I'm heading into town for the rest of the day."

"Right. Good luck with those building permits. Hope Rebecca's job interview goes well."

"She'll be just fine as can be."

Graham froze. It was another Emily phrase, this time spoken with the exact same amount of Texas drawl. The exact same inflection. He looked at Trey again. No resemblance, none at all. Emily would have to be an extra-tall woman, or Trey would have to have a slender build. Emily's eyes were dark. Trey's were light.

Luke was the cousin who ran Emily's ranch. She'd talked about Luke a lot. Luke was going to hire a new hand. But there was a brother—owned a third of the land—hadn't bothered to come home for ten years, not until Luke's wedding just weeks ago. The brother's name, had she mentioned it? Trey had sounded so familiar when Gus said it.

Graham looked at the contract. Trey had signed it *James Waterson III*. Right—this ranch owner was Waterson, not Davis. Trey himself looked as hard-core cowboy as Gus did. He wasn't a man who'd been out of ranching for ten years. This was a million-dollar cattle operation, not a family ranch.

Graham hadn't just taken Emily's job.

"Gus, I'm here to take that job."

Emily looked herself in the eye as she stood in front of the bathroom mirror and braided her freshly washed hair. She was feeling calm after her nap and her shower. She just needed to practice her opening line. Once she spit it out, all the rest would flow.

"Gus, I'm the new hand Uncle James needs here on the ranch."

For working cattle, Emily usually parted her hair in the middle and made two braids, one on each side. That was easy to do, and it kept all of her hair out of her face and off the back of her neck from dawn to dusk when she chased down stragglers as they drove the herd to the far hundred. Now she looked in the mirror and worried that it made her look too young.

She undid the braids and started over. One braid straight down her back would look more mature.

One braid to the side was for bed. After midnight, it had been for Graham.

For Graham, who was on her team.

Graham, who believed in her.

She took a breath and looked in the mirror. She could do this. She deserved this job. And she would call Graham tonight and tell him she'd gotten her job and her new place to live, so he didn't need to worry about her. He was out in the middle of nowhere, but maybe the satellite gods would be kind and bounce her signal to his phone. She wanted to hear his voice.

"Gus, let's talk about where I fit on the James Hill."

That would work, because she did fit on the James Hill. Gus had practically raised her to be part of the James Hill. She finished her braid, gathered up last night's clothes, stopped in the mudroom to stomp on her boots and put everything back in her truck. It was time to walk to Gus's office. This was it.

She looked around, but there was nobody else at the house, so she took out the Marine Corps jacket and, one more time, buried her face in it. He was coming back for her. Someday.

She wished someday wasn't three months away.

Chapter Fifteen

"Ain't you a little old to be a greenhorn?"

Aren't you a little young to be so cocky?

Graham ignored the ranch hand who was supposed to be helping him. He opened the ATV's drain plug and let the oil start draining into the drain pan. Pretty elementary stuff, but apparently this young cowboy thought it was a big test of manhood that the new guy—the greenhorn—might fail. He was watching Graham like a hawk. What he wasn't doing was helping.

"Hand me the filter wrench," Graham said.

"You're the greenhorn. You do the fetching and carrying."

Graham was too old for this crap. Too old, and too experienced. He stayed where he was, on one knee by the ATV, and wiped the oil off his fingers with the rag, taking his time. "Here's the problem, Sid. You stuck the filter wrench under your ass when you sat on that bench. Either you want to watch me search through the toolbox for some-thing you know isn't there, or you want me to come and stick my hand under you to get the wrench." He looked from his hand to the cowboy. "Either way, Sid, you got the wrong man."

He finished wiping his fingers off and tossed the rag at Sid, who had no choice but to catch it if he didn't want it to hit his chest. "Hand me the filter wrench."

Sid threw it more than tossed it, but that was all right. Let him be pissed that he got bested. Graham caught the wrench and started loosening the oil filter.

"Just testing you," Sid said, sounding like a petulant child. "Don't be touching me. Where'd you come from, anyway?"

"Chicago."

Graham had planned on three months of silence. Three months of being alone to hear his own empty thoughts echo in his empty head. *Not happening.*

"What'd you do in Chicago?"

"I dropped out of college." Graham hid a smile at the way Sid nodded in approval. "How about you? Have you been here long?"

"James hired me last roundup. Old James, not the foot-ball James. That one goes by Trey."

"Yeah, I got that. I haven't met the older James yet."

"Probably won't before roundup. He and his wife are off on one trip or t'other most of the time. Go to Timbuktu or something."

Very precisely, without thinking about anything else, Graham took the new oil filter out of its cardboard box. He kept the box in his palm. It was perfectly empty, like his brain. He knew nothing. He wanted to know nothing.

My aunt and uncle travel around the world. The mem-ory was clear, even the way Emily had stood between his knees when she'd said it, barefoot on the cold ground, excitedly explaining her plan.

Graham dragged his sleeve across his mouth. *Trey*. Emily had said her other cousin's name was Trey. Graham couldn't keep his mind blank enough.

"How about Luke?" Graham asked. *Go ahead and hit me with it*.

Sid did. "You'll see more of him than you want to. Luke runs the place. He's on some hoity-toity honeymoon with his hoity-toity bride right now."

He kept talking, but Graham didn't hear a thing over the roaring in his head. Of course Sid hadn't said *never heard of anyone named Luke*. Of course not. God-effing-dammit. *Holy frigging crackers*.

A Texas girl's idea of a family ranch was wildly different than his own.

He needed to keep a cool head. He had no choice but to adapt to the change of plans. There was a definite upside: he'd see Emily, and he'd see her often. His heart wouldn't be so far away.

But if so, he should have already seen her. She should have beaten him by two hours or more to Gus's office. She could have decided to drive back to Austin to confront her mother first. He could see Emily wanting to get the hardest part out of the way. He hoped she'd thought to pack her things in her truck before her parents had a chance to throw her out. She wouldn't obey Graham's order—his request—to call him if she needed help, but he should never have left his phone in his SUV, signal or no signal.

"Fancy." Sid was suddenly intent on something outside the door of the ATV shed. "Mm, mm, mm. That there is some fancy meat walkin'."

Graham hardly needed to turn around to see what was making Sid lick his chops.

Emily was walking past the shed, oblivious to their presence. The Texas winter sunshine was as beautiful on her as the moonlight. How could he feel this irrationally happy to see her again? It was like seeing her after years instead of hours. The pleasure of it hurt.

He stood to watch her pass, same as Sid. Emily wore a plaid shirt, mostly red, a muted color like the barns. It was tucked into jeans that were belted with a silver Western buckle that reflected sunlight for one second of sparkle. The decorative boots had been replaced by a pair that looked plain and sturdy. Then she was past the shed and he was admiring the view from behind. Her braid was still wet, but she'd redone it so that it was hanging down her back, as straight as her spine.

"Mmm-hmm, I'd tap that," Sid said. "I'd tap that hard and I'd tap that long."

It would be so easy to break Sid in half. So very easy.

Graham couldn't give away his relationship with Emily, not without talking to her first. How would she want to handle this new situation?

"I've had my eye on her for a while," Sid said, frowning at him. "Don't get any ideas, greenhorn. I got dibs."

No, Sid, you don't. Not in this lifetime.

Then Graham remembered that Emily wasn't just out walking to take in the mild weather. She was headed directly for the barn that held Gus's office. She was going to get her job.

Even the Marine Corps didn't have enough curse words to express Graham's feelings as he quickly screwed on the new filter and poured in new oil through a funnel.

"You do the other ATV and clean up," he ordered Sid as he headed out of the shed.

"Hey. No, man, you're the green—"

"Give it a rest. I've got something to do."

Something he dreaded.

Nothing to be nervous about. It's only the first day of the rest of your life.

Emily took a deep breath and knocked on the door frame to the foreman's office. Gus always left the door open.

"Emily. Well, aren't you a sight for sore eyes?"

"It's good to be back, thank you. Gus, let's talk about where I fit—"

"Hardly got to talk to you last time you were here, what with all the wedding goings-on and the ice storm and all. How's college treating you?" He kicked back in his desk chair, ready for a talk.

"Well, I'm done with college, actually." She'd never in her life felt so nervous to talk to the foreman.

Gus squinted at her. "Did I not get the invitation to the party? I know your mama's gonna throw a graduation party."

"I've got one class left, but I'll take it this summer online and get my diploma in September. I don't need to spend an entire semester in Oklahoma just to take that one class."

"Huh. Thought you said *done*."

Emily knew what that skeptical sound and that squinty look meant. Gus had always made all the cousins tell the truth, the whole truth, and nothing but the truth. "I'm not technically done, I know. But for all practical purposes, I am. It's almost a formality right now, and that is the absolute truth. So, Gus, let's talk about—"

"September now? I thought it was going to be May."

"September." Exasperation made her ditch her opening line. "Gus, I'm trying to ask you something."

"Shoot."

She looked at the man who'd hoisted her onto her first pony and felt a very real affection for him. Everything was going to be okay. "You know I always wanted to be you when I grew up, right?"

"You'll never be as pretty as me, but you might have even more horse sense than I do. You and Trey, the both of you, ever since you were itty-bitty."

Emily smiled patiently. Trey was long gone from the ranch, having nothing to do with it as an adult, but she supposed Gus had fond memories of their childhoods. The only thing she'd seen Trey ride when he came back for the wedding was an ATV—although he'd used that to save Rebecca from freezing to death in an ice storm, so she had to give Trey major kudos for saving a life.

"Thanks, Gus. You've taught me horses and more. I'm here because I want to keep learning about ranch management from you."

Gus stood up from his desk and looked around his office as if she'd asked him for a stapler or something and he was ready to hand it to her. "What do you need to know?"

"Nothing specific. I mean I'm ready to work here year-round now. College really is over, and I want to work for the man who'll always be prettier than me. I was in the kitchen with Uncle James and Luke last month when they decided to hire another ranch hand. I can save you the time and trouble of putting out an ad. You won't waste time interviewing slackers. I'd like the job."

"What job? Ranch hand?"

"That's me."

"I can't believe what I'm hearing."

Emily held on to her pleasant expression, but Gus wasn't looking so friendly. He got serious, fast.

"You should know better than to ask me, young lady. You should know better."

Graham didn't run to the barn, but he came close. He walked in the open door at a good clip, temporarily blinded in the relative darkness after the bright Texas sun. *Left to right, check the—*

Screw it. The stalls would be impossible for one man to clear.

Not clear. He went to get Emily, anyway.

His rubber-soled boots made no noise on the concrete, and the door to Gus's office was open, so he became an accidental eavesdropper, stopping when he heard Emily's voice.

"The timing is great. Luke needs the help, you need the help."

"Now, all that might be true, but—"

"There's no *might* about it, Gus. I can do anything you need. You know I can, but I'm not asking for the high end of the pay scale. The starter will be enough for the first contract. I need the room more than the pay."

"Room? *Room?* You aren't expecting me to put you in that bunkhouse with a bunch of men."

Graham felt the pause. He walked to the door and saw Emily's back as she faced Gus over the desk. The set of her shoulders was familiar. She was about to set the record straight. He almost smiled.

"Actually, I am. I'm expecting you to put me in that bunkhouse as a ranch hand with other ranch hands. It's part of the standard compensation. It's got nothing to do with women or men. Besides, I wouldn't be the first woman you've hired who goes to live in that bunkhouse."

"The last one we hired ended up getting married."

"Which is not against the law. Refusing to hire someone just because she's female is." But Emily stopped there. Her tone softened. "C'mon, Gus, it was a nice wedding. Shelley and Steve make a great team, or you wouldn't still be hiring them to get the cattle to auction every year."

"Your mama has higher expectations for you than living in an RV with some two-bit itinerate cowboy."

"Ouch. Poor Steve."

Graham smiled to himself. *Way to go, Emily.* She was using humor instead of getting sucked into an argument.

Gus continued to expound on all the reasons the bunkhouse was unsuitable, from the beer-stained furniture to the vulgar language she might hear, none of it, in Gus's opinion, fit for a lady. Graham didn't think Gus was doing it on purpose, but he was derailing the conversation, sending it off on a sidetrack when Emily had come to be hired for her ranching skills.

Emily slid her hands into her back pockets. "I know you mean well, Gus, but I'm not the helpless kind of female."

"I know that."

"I don't think you do." She paused, and Graham wondered if she'd just remembered telling him the same thing on the side of the road. "I've been around cowboys my whole life. I know what to expect. I surely don't need some kind of extra-fine lady sofa to sit on. This notion of chivalry actually can hurt more than help. If you kept me out of the bunkhouse for my own good, it would leave me homeless, which is worse."

"Why would you ever be homeless? What does your mama have to say about all this?"

"I'm twenty-two. You don't need my mother's permission to hire me, and I don't need her permission to ask for the job."

"Emily Dawn—"

"But since you've known her a long time, let me tell you what's going on there. I promised her I'd get a bachelor's degree and I'm keeping that promise. In order to do that, I need a job, so I can afford that last class. I've got to get a job, Gus, and there is nowhere else I'd rather work."

She shoots; she scores. Graham was proud of her. Impressed with her. Hell, he was ready to hire her.

Gus wasn't. "You're already free to work here as much as you like. You always do, every break you get from school."

"Yes, but I don't get paid for my work. I need the salary. I need the room. You'll get your money's worth out of me, and you know that."

"I won't ever hire you, young lady. You're not a ranch hand, you'll never be a ranch hand and you should know that."

Emily was silent. She stayed just as she was, shoulders back, confident, but Graham could practically hear her hope bursting. She'd been so certain that if a plan was reasonable, it would work. He'd tried to temper her expectations. He'd warned her to remember both possible outcomes: either it would work, or it wouldn't.

She wasn't ready for the *wouldn't*. He could see Gus's face beyond her, and a more stubborn expression on a man's face couldn't exist. The answer was no, fair or not.

His uncle had seen him outside the door, of course. He motioned him in now. "I've already hired the new ranch hand. Emily, let me introduce you to Benjamin Graham."

He saw her little jump at the name. She whirled around to face him, and for a second, for one precious second, her eyes lit up with joy at the sight of him. Then the implications came crashing through her. Every emotion passed over that expressive, beautiful face, until she settled on being...horrified.

"You—you *took my job*?"

"Emily." But he could only greet her without revealing their relationship.

"What are you doing here?" She was baffled. She turned back to Gus. Turned back to Graham. "You're supposed to be out in the middle of nowhere. This isn't nowhere."

"I know that now." He wondered if she realized she'd just revealed that they'd already met and discussed where he was supposed to be.

"What have you done, Graham?" The despair, the betrayal in her voice tore at him. "You heard me say the job hadn't been advertised yet, so you came here first? You decided to beat me to it? That is so low."

"No, that's not it."

But she'd turned to Gus. "And you hired him? Over me?" Her horror gave way to fury. "He knows nothing about ranching. Nothing. He's from *Chicago*. I'm the cowboy you've trained for how long? Fifteen years? And you chose him over me?"

Now Gus was the one in shock, clearly wondering how Emily knew anything about Graham.

Emily made no allowance for Gus's shock. "I mean, the bunkhouse—you can't be so old-fashioned that you think it's more important to be a man than to actually be a cowboy. Just being a man doesn't make him better than me. Not when you know how good I am at the job."

"Emily, I'm sorry," Graham began.

She threw her hand in his direction in disgust, a hand that shook with emotion as much as it ever had from freezing lake water. "You've never even ridden a horse, and you got my job."

The cat was out of the bag now. They knew one another, no pretending otherwise, so Graham wasn't going to stand still and watch her go through so many terrible emotions.

She looked pale, frail, cold. He crossed the distance between them and put his hand on her waist, as if he were going to get her out of a bad situation.

Her first instinct was to trust him. She grabbed him, a fistful of shirt, and steadied herself. But after one breath, she pushed away, palm flat against his body.

"Don't—" she said in a whisper. "Just don't."

She stood taller. Lifted her chin. Leveled a look on Gus and spoke stiffly. "I'll never be a ranch hand, you said. I know you're wrong. All I want is to be a rancher, so I'll need to find work elsewhere, but I'll need a reference. You could vouch for my horse sense. My experience on cattle drives. Running the baler. Can I rely on you for that much?"

Gus's brow knit in consternation. "First of all, young lady, I didn't hire Benjamin just because he's male. He's a veteran, and he's strong and he's smart. I don't appreciate you thinking I'd put someone on the James Hill who was useless."

"But I am your nephew," Graham said, watching Emily to see if she'd figured that out yet, although Gus's last name was Montano. "I appreciate you giving me the opportunity, but I wouldn't have gotten it if I wasn't your nephew."

"Ranches are all about family." Gus leaned forward, knuckles on his desk, white with pressure as he stayed intent on Emily. "Family, did you hear me? There is one reason I'll never hire you, and it isn't because of your skills or even because you're a young girl. It's because you're family, and not just any family. You belong to the family that owns this land. I know our great country is supposed to be built on all men being created equal, but it ain't that way in cattle country. Men that own their own grass outrank men that gotta buy their hay. Cattlemen outrank foremen like me. The foreman outranks the ranch hands." He threw Graham a look. "The hands outrank the greenhorn, and so on. Miss Emily—do you remember how I always called you Miss Emily? Miss Emily should know that I'm not going to take a Waterson and make her a ranch hand on her own gosh-danged-blessed land."

Emily stared Gus down. "I'm not a Waterson."

"You're James and Jessie Waterson's niece. You're the closest thing to a sister that Luke and Trey have. I don't appreciate you expecting me to treat you like you're some ranch hand looking for starter pay and a room. You're crazier than a bull-bat if you think I'm going to put Luke Waterson's sister in the bunkhouse for him to find when he gets back."

Graham understood, as he had while listening to Emily last night, that he didn't know enough about her family or about ranching to be able to advise anyone in this situation. But his uncle was squaring off with the woman who had his heart, the two of them bristling like a couple of wolves about to go at it, so Graham needed to defuse the situation. Immediately.

Emily didn't want any softness from him. Since he was a little behind her, he could gesture impatiently at his uncle without her seeing it. *Sit down, back off.* Graham hooked his foot around the leg of a straight chair and kicked it closer to the desk, the least tender way he could possibly offer Emily a seat.

It worked. Once Gus sat, she sat. There was nowhere for Graham to sit, but that was fine. He crossed his arms over his chest and stayed beside her. *I'm on your side.* Even though he'd taken her job.

She glanced up at him and did a little double take. "I don't need a bodyguard. I'll take Gus out if he takes a swing at me."

Gus snorted. "Only because I've got forty years on

you. If I were forty years younger..." He trailed off and looked at Graham. "Well, if I were forty years younger, I'd be him. And when I was young, if I met a pretty spit-fire like yourself, the last thing on my mind would be fighting. I'd—I'd..." He looked from Graham to Emily and back. "Never mind what I'd do. How do you two know each other?"

Neither of them spoke for a moment too long.

Emily went with the truth. "He was at Keller's last night."

"Keller's? Heard there was a fight. They called police out and it was a mess all ways to Sunday."

"We waited it out on the patio," Graham said. It was true enough. "We had a lot of time to talk." Also true.

"We talked about this job," Emily added, "but he never said his uncle's name was Gus."

She said it through clenched teeth. Since the subject was serving the purpose of distracting her and Gus from tearing each other's throats out—and since Graham had his own grievance—he stated his case, too. "You said your family owned twenty dairy cows."

Gus snorted at that.

"I did not."

"Did so."

"Did not." She pressed her lips together when she re-alized where that was going. "I said we had twenty dairy cows when we lived in San Antonio. That was the smallest, tiniest bit of ranching in my life, but it was still ranching."

Gus snorted at that, too, but he seemed satisfied with how they knew one another, because he sat forward with his hands clasped together on the desk. He no longer had white knuckles and that angry stare.

Mission accomplished.

Emily sat back in her chair and crossed her arms like

Graham as she picked up her gauntlet once more. "Okay. Let's say you're right. I'm not greenhorn. I'm way too knowledgeable about this ranch to ever be a greenhorn."

I hear you. Don't rub it in.

"Luke wants Trey and Uncle James to step up. You hired Graham here for Uncle James, but what about Trey? He's supposed to hire someone, too, since he's never around, but hiring two greenhorns isn't really going to do the trick, is it?

"It seems to me that you and Luke and even Uncle James seem to have some kind of superstition about family being on the land. If I'm family, like you say, I'll represent Trey. Then Luke can live part-time in Austin, and there will still be a Waterson on the land. Between me and Luke, family will always be around."

Emily grew more excited with each sentence. "Since you think I'm some kind of ranch royalty that can't live in the bunkhouse, I'll live in the ranch house. That'll make you happy. Luke built himself that new addition. I can use Trey's old room and not be in their way."

Emily had no quit in her. She'd taken in Gus's objections and come up with a new plan that should satisfy everyone.

She looked up at him, just to see if he liked her idea—he knew that was behind her half smile, the same as it had been last night when she'd told him all her plans. Too quickly, she remembered that he was in the job she'd wanted. Her smile died before it got started, and she turned back to Gus.

Gus was looking a little sad. No—it was pity. "Emily, sugar, before you get your heart set on that, you need to talk to Trey about filling in for Trey."

"Only Watersons can hire Watersons?" Emily rolled her eyes a little. "Okay, then. Trey lives in Oklahoma, but I have to drive back to Tech to move out of my campus apartment, anyway. I'll take a detour and go see him in person. We'll get it all worked out. This will be a better solution than me just taking that three-month contract."

"Sugar," Gus started. Hesitated.

Graham had that moment of emptiness again, the one that came before he forced himself to see the truth. He hadn't wanted to see that the James Hill was Emily's family ranch, and now he didn't want to see...

Her plan couldn't work. Trey wasn't in Oklahoma. He was here, after an absence of ten years, signing contracts like the owner he was. Emily didn't know it yet.

Emily, sweet girl, it would have been a good solution. I'm so sorry...

"Sugar, I mean that Trey is going to take Trey's place. He's moving back home. You just missed him, in fact. He went into Austin to meet up with Rebecca and get some building permits and such."

"He's back?"

Gus was silent.

"It's been ten years." Emily sounded stunned.

"Well now, seems that once he set foot back on his land, he decided not to leave again."

"He didn't even recognize me when he came for the wedding. He hadn't seen me since I was in middle school." Abruptly, she stood up, her chair scraping across the floor for a few noisy inches. "Right when I'm finally done with college, right when I could start living here full-time, *now* Trey's back? *Now* he's decided he gives a damn about this ranch?"

"Trey's going to marry Rebecca and settle down right here, where he belongs."

Graham didn't know who Rebecca was, but Emily gasped at this news, too. "He just met her. We all just met her. How could he possibly be that much in love with her?"

You stole my heart before sunrise, sweet girl. It happens.

The girl who had Graham's heart didn't have the heart to keep fighting this battle. In silence, in defeat, she turned to leave. Graham was standing between her and the door. He uncrossed his arms, but he couldn't think of the right thing to say.

"You're not off the grid, Graham," she whispered. "You're just in my way."

She stepped around him and left.

Chapter Sixteen

Graham followed.

He didn't interrupt her silent thoughts. He didn't try to touch her, but he walked beside her. She'd been his lover just hours ago. He wasn't going to leave her when she was grappling with the *wouldn't*.

"I don't want to talk to you," she said too calmly.

"I know. You don't have to."

She walked up to the split rail fence of the horse pasture and allowed herself to deflate a little, hugging the top rail and setting one boot on the bottom rail.

Graham put his boot on the bottom rail, too.

That seemed to annoy her. "What are you doing?"

It was an excellent question. He wasn't doing anything he'd expected to be doing this morning. He wasn't doing anything he could have predicted while sitting in a classroom, or at an office desk, or in a sandbag bunker. But ever since he'd seen Emily's face in the light at that bar, his own life had started to take shape. He was breathing again, waking up, seeing in color.

It wasn't the type of answer she was looking for, but Graham rested against the fence and spoke the truth. "You know how you never want to leave this ranch? I never want to leave you."

She sucked in a breath, short and sharp, like he'd pricked her with a needle again.

"I didn't steal your job," he said. "It was offered to me just after Christmas. You decided to apply last night, but it had already been filled for weeks."

She was silent. She wouldn't look at him, but she must have felt him looking at her, because she did give him a regal nod worthy of ranching royalty.

"Regardless, Gus wouldn't have hired you because of the family connection."

"That's what he said, but we'll never know what would have happened if the position was empty." Then she ducked between the fence rails and started walking away from him—or maybe, he hoped, it was less that she was walking away from him and more that she was walking toward the horses. He'd thought of the horses as being untouchable, isolated on their side of the fence like exotic animals in a zoo, but Emily strolled among them, putting out her hand to pat one or two as she passed them. Old friends.

One horse seemed particularly alert to her presence, lifting his head in her direction, twitching his ears. She stopped and petted his nose, stroked his neck, combed her fingers through his mane. As Graham watched, she simply gripped a handful of the horse's mane, gave the smallest hop and a kick, and vaulted onto the back of the horse. She landed so lightly, it looked like the most natural, easy thing to do.

He didn't see her tap her boot heels into the horse's side

or give any kind of verbal command, but the horse started walking directly to a gate on the far side of the pasture. Emily leaned down to open it, ride through, close it. Graham missed the command again, but the horse broke into a run as Emily bent close to its neck, riding bareback, just that handful of mane in her hand as she disappeared down the rise.

Gus spoke from close behind him. "She's quite a horsewoman."

It was beautiful. It was humbling. Emily had a whole way of life Graham knew nothing about. "I've never seen anything like that."

"You rarely do."

"Where's she going?"

"She won't go too far, not without a bridle. Let her go. It'll be good for her."

Let her go? Graham had no choice. How did his uncle think he'd follow her? Emily called her own shots, as Graham had told Mr. Schumer just last night, but she lived in a world where men seemed to think they were allowing her to do things—allowing her to buy beer when they knew she was of legal age, allowing her to ride a horse when she was already its master, allowing her to work for free during every college break, when they probably relied on her. As an outsider, Graham could see it. In this ranching world, he suspected the men did not. But Emily did, and it was wearing her down.

His uncle took her place at the railing. "Now, would you care to explain to me if you were under some covers at a hotel with a heated swimming pool before you met her at Keller's Bar, or after?"

Graham ran the pad of his thumb over his bottom lip. Emily had only told Gus about the bar. The pond, the dock and the rope, those were secrets between them, and always would be. *Graham and Emily, down by the lake that night.*

"She's the boss's sister," Gus said.

"Cousin."

"Either way, it's asking for trouble. How much trouble there's already been is what I'd like to know."

Graham kept his eye on the spot where she'd disappeared. "I meant what I said in there about being grateful you brought me on board at this ranch, but I've been on my own for too long. I don't account for my whereabouts or my covers or anything else to anyone. Not even to the uncle I owe this job to."

"I've known her since she was yea-high in pink cowgirl boots. It would be a sin to break that girl's heart."

"I didn't. This ranch did."

Graham pushed off the fence and turned back to the barn. It was time to go shovel out stalls.

Graham's shoulder withstood the shoveling well enough. He didn't have to lift the pitchfork high to toss manure into a wheelbarrow, and the constant motion of sifting through hay from one stall to another, stall after stall, kept the joint too warm to freeze up. He was going to feel it tomorrow morning, though. Sleep made his shoulder stiff.

Sid was useless once more after another attempt to haze him. He'd tried to make Graham use a garden hoe, then a snow shovel to clean out the first stall, but both tools failed the common sense test. Graham had needed to set Sid straight again before he'd been handed the right pitchfork. Sid had the lazier, easier job of watching Graham clean out the stall, then coming after him and tossing in some fresh hay apathetically.

"Fancy."

Graham stopped what he was doing.

Sid wolf whistled, but being the sad sack he was, he kept it low enough for only Graham to catch. He didn't have the guts to actually whistle at the boss's cousin.

"Mm, mm, mm..."

Graham smacked the pitchfork into Sid's hands. "Finish up."

"Hey, man." But that was the extent of Sid's objection this time. He was learning.

Graham went to the open barn door to see Emily returning, riding her horse at a gentle walk. Uncle Gus was waiting for her, rope in his hand. He looped the rope over the horse's neck as Emily neatly dismounted. Graham couldn't hear what was said, not really, but if his lip reading was good enough, Gus had said, "He's waiting for you."

Emily turned to look for...him. Graham knew it in his bones. He was the man on her mind.

But Gus had been talking about Trey, who'd been leaning against the side of a building, watching his cousin ride in from the land beyond the pasture. No doubt, Gus had filled Trey in on the situation when he'd returned from Austin. Emily dusted her hands off, Gus took the horse away, and Trey simply walked up to his cousin, put his arm over her shoulders and started walking her back to the house, the Waterson house, where the ranch royalty lived.

Graham didn't give in to the heartache. He knew what he'd seen. Emily had looked for him.

It kept him going long enough to finish the work for the day, to return to the barracks—the bunkhouse—to take a shower after being awake for thirty-six hours. When he would have fallen into bed, instead he dressed with some care, a collared shirt and fresh jeans, and he brush-shined his black boots, because military men didn't walk around with dusty boots, not even on a ranch.

He walked a mile to the main house in the last of the twilight. Trey answered his knock.

"May I speak to Emily?"

"She's not here. She went back to her mother's house."

Graham let that sink in a moment. It was possible Emily had just felt like a third wheel with Trey and someone new named Rebecca, so she'd gone back to her home to sleep tonight.

That wasn't why she'd gone, and he knew it.

She'd gone back to confront her mother about the master's degree. Emily didn't know how to not fight for what she wanted. She had so much heart. She had his heart, too, whether she needed it or wanted it, and he didn't like not knowing where it was.

"Is there any chance you'll give me that address?"

"I don't have it."

Trey wasn't lying. He was too straightforward, too much like Emily. Graham should have seen the resemblance right away. He just hadn't been ready to.

"If this is the part where you warn me off dating your cousin, it's unnecessary. I know I'm wrong for her." There were too many gaps between what he should have done, what he had done, what he wanted to do. "I'm still going to check on her."

"Nothing's a secret on this ranch for long, but if you haven't been informed, I'll tell you that I haven't seen Emily in ten years. The Emily I knew had braces on her teeth and tried to play some god-awful boy band music in the barn. Looks like she's all grown up now to me, so what one grown-up does with another is none of my business, as long as the ranch runs smoothly."

Graham nodded.

"As long as you're not cruel. Or careless." Trey sized him up. "Then it would get interesting."

Graham wasn't cocky enough to predict an easy victory over Trey in a fistfight. *Interesting* meant Trey felt the same about him.

Graham had no intention of letting anything get to that point. He wasn't cruel. He knew what cruelty looked like, bloody and merciless and sick. Combat had, once more, stolen his ability to claim anything else was cruel for the rest of his life. Intentionally breaking a heart was low, but it wasn't inhuman cruelty.

When it came to being careless with a lover's emotions, Graham couldn't get out of his own head long enough to be careless. He'd been too intentional every step with Emily, but he was glad Emily had a cousin like Trey in her corner, if there were another man in her future.

The possibility of future men, fumbling idiots, made him angry.

"All right," Graham said. "Good night."

"Work should be light tomorrow. Good time for you to get up on a horse."

Emily had promised him his first ride.

But Emily didn't work here. Graham did, and Trey owned the place, so Graham just nodded, repeated his good-night and walked back to his new home, alone.

Twenty-four hours ago, it had been all he wanted. Now, it was all wrong.

Emily knew she was a failure.

She hated it.

Worse, she hated that Graham was the one person in the world who would know exactly how far short of her goals she'd fallen. She returned to the James Hill in the morning wanting only to saddle up a horse and disappear. Instead, she'd found Graham in the barn's center aisle, along with Sid and Bonner. The two hands were snorting and laughing up their sleeves, taking the saddle off an impatient, young gelding.

"Okay, now let's see you do it." They hopped up onto stall doors, ready to enjoy themselves at the greenhorn's expense.

Emily tried to be invisible as she kept her favorite mare in her stall and began brushing her quickly. Then Emily smoothed a saddle pad over the horse's back and turned to her saddle. She laid the stirrup and straps over one side of the saddle and hefted it—swung it with some momentum, really, for saddles were heavy—over her horse's back, then rocked it a bit, making sure it was seated correctly.

She stole a look down the aisle. Graham had plopped a saddle on the gelding and was tightening the girth, but he'd forgotten the pad. Sid and Bonner were loving it. "Yeah, good job. Go ahead and mount up, see how it feels."

The gelding would be confused that someone was mounting him in the building, a stranger at that. He'd be confused why he was being mounted while wearing a halter instead of a bridle, and he'd be unhappy with the saddle rubbing directly on him without a pad. He might even buck to get the saddle and rider off. Graham wouldn't know how to keep a seat on a bucking horse. It was a huge challenge for Emily, and she was a top rider with a lifetime of experience.

They were standing on the concrete center aisle. If Graham were bucked off...man versus concrete...

She could hardly look at Graham, as embarrassed as she was that he'd witnessed her humiliation at being turned down for the job she'd bragged she was perfect for, but she had no problem glaring at the idiots messing with the horse. She left her mare in the stall and walked into the aisle.

"Sid! Bonner."

They both looked her way, surprised.

"You two don't know how to train a cowboy to save your lives."

They tried to splutter some weak objections—*not a cowboy, he's a greenhorn; meant no harm*. She spoke right over their excuses. "If you had any sense, you wouldn't let the horse learn to hate that saddle, not one single time, not for your own entertainment." She was truly angry; horses weren't for entertainment. "I get that you want to get your jollies at the greenhorn's expense, but you can't do it at the horse's expense. It's not your horse to screw around with, is it?"

They wouldn't meet her eye. They just sat sullenly, awkwardly, on their perch on the stable doors.

It was, she realized, *her* horse, as far as they were concerned. Just as Gus had said, she was part of *the* family, the owners' family. The two ranch hands were as embarrassed at being busted by her as they would have been getting caught by Luke—or Trey, now.

"This horse is part of the James Hill. If you don't respect that, you don't need to be part of the James Hill. You're more easily replaced than the horse."

"We wouldn't have let the greenhorn mount up on a bad saddle," Bonner muttered, his halfhearted attempt to defend himself.

"Bull." Emily had been raised here. She knew when a cowboy was full of it. "Go see Gus. Tell him you're available to do something else."

While they were still in earshot, she snapped at Graham. "Get that saddle off. You're not riding this horse today."

He started loosening the cinch, but he winked at her. He *winked*.

"Don't w—" She had to stop. Sid and Bonner were

still in hearing distance. She settled for a scowl. *Don't wink at me.*

"Well done," he said quietly, so only she could hear. Then he went to lift the saddle. She didn't imagine that flash of pain on his face and the way his left hand slipped.

"Are you hurt?" Dumb question. Obviously, he was. She was going to kill Sid and Bonner.

"No, fine." He lifted the saddle barely high enough to clear the gelding's backbone and pulled it to his chest. "What's next?"

"That all depends on how badly you're hurt."

He was surprised at that. "I'm not."

She was just as surprised that he'd lie. "Your left shoulder or hand or something."

"It's fine." He shook his left arm out, keeping the saddle over only his right arm—she couldn't do that, because the saddles were heavy enough that she needed both arms to carry them.

A sexual memory hit her, Graham's bare chest and arms, muscles that flexed in the moonlight. Of course he could hold the saddle with one arm—but he was human, and it was heavy.

"Set the saddle down." She waited until he did, and she watched how he didn't use his left arm much at all. "Listen, I can guess that your military background means you keep going when you're injured, but you're on a ranch now. The goal around here is to keep everything healthy. If a horse was favoring his left leg, I wouldn't work him until I knew what was going on. I'm not going to work you if you're hurt."

He was silent.

Suddenly, it was just Graham and Emily, talking all night long, and she had standards when it came to conversation.

"Silence isn't an answer, Graham."

He sighed, extra loud. "If you're waiting until my left shoulder improves, you'll never get a day's work out of me. It's an old injury."

"How bad?"

He put his left arm around her waist and pulled her closer. "It works well enough to do the important things."

He bent his head, paused over her parted lips and then he kissed her. Nothing else mattered. It felt like she was kissing him for the first time in a year, *finally, oh finally, welcome home*.

She felt herself melt into him, felt that sexual pull, but it was all mixed up in a roller coaster of emotions. The kiss brought back all the elation she'd felt by the lake, all her high hopes—all the hopes that had been dashed. She clung to him harder as he kissed her, but she still felt some of the shock that Graham had the job she wanted. She couldn't forget the humiliation of Gus lecturing her or her mother's ultimatums last night. She had to go back to college.

Graham was going to be so disappointed in her. She wasn't anything like the woman she'd thought she was at the lake.

She ended the kiss and backed into the horse, then automatically apologized as if she'd backed into a person in a crowded bar. "Oh, sorry."

She tried to laugh it off. "I suppose you would advise me not to apologize to the horse."

Graham didn't laugh.

Emily concentrated fiercely on the saddle at his feet. His shoulder—this had all started with his shoulder. "Let me see you put the saddle on him."

"Emily."

Oh, she hated that *be sensible* tone of voice. It was all she'd heard last night from her mother and stepfather. "I want to see you put the saddle on the horse. I'm not just looking at how your shoulder works. I'm looking to see how many bad habits Sid and Bonner managed to instill in a short amount of time."

"Ah, Emily."

Well, that was a little better. Less paternal. More like a lover.

"Try not to be mad at me for taking this job," Graham said quietly, so the words stayed between them and didn't echo through the barn. "Gus offered it to me weeks ago, not yesterday morning."

"Yes, you told me that. I'd rather not talk about that little job interview. I wish you hadn't been there."

"Why not?"

Because it showed you all my flaws. I'm too young, too weak. I got chewed out by your uncle. She wished she wasn't so attracted to Graham. It would be better to just walk away and find a new boyfriend back at college.

As if. She wasn't going to find another man who so instantly and totally appealed to her like Graham did, and she knew it. Her future would be a pretty lonely one.

Sadness made her as grouchy as sexual frustration had. "Just put the saddle on the horse. Get a pad first, so you're doing it right. You can't slide the saddle up and over, because the pad would slide off. Most people toss the heavier saddles up and over."

You can lift yours and set it down. Not everyone is tall and strong, and did you have to be handsome, too?

Graham had no problem lifting the saddle until the last few inches of height. He tried to be all stoic about it, but his left hand let go of the pommel and caught the saddle lower, a little juggling move that let him keep raising the saddle until he could set it on the horse's back.

She shrugged. "Actually, that works fine."

"Great."

"Now take it all off."

He slid her a look, a smile. "That's what she said."

She wanted to roll her eyes and laugh with him. She really did, but she saw him shake out his left arm, just a little bit, before reaching for the saddle. He was in pain.

She wasn't the fearless woman she'd pretended to be yesterday at dawn, but he had been her lover once in the moonlight, and she'd never forget it. She didn't want him to be in pain. Ever.

The gelding reflected her turmoil as she held his halter. He wasn't a very patient horse in the first place, which made him a terrible choice for this type of rudimentary lesson. He'd been shifting and blowing and tossing his head all along, but now Emily backed him up a step by pushing on his chest to remind him not to get pushy with a human. She tapped his hoof with her boot until he moved his leg so that he was standing squarely on all four feet.

"Okay. Go ahead and take the saddle off."

Graham didn't move.

"What?"

"Remember what I said about the schoolteacher tone being a turn-on? This horse trainer thing you do is killing me. Damn it, Emily." He looked down the aisle quickly and then kissed her, only his mouth on her mouth for one hot second, a hard claim on her body.

While a wave of purely physical desire flooded her in the wake of that kiss, Graham grabbed the saddle and lifted it off the horse. He bent to set it on the floor.

He was in pain. He could lift the saddle, but he was in pain. Had he been in pain last night at any point? Had he made her laugh when she hadn't known?

"Tell me about your shoulder."

He hesitated, then let go of the saddle and stood. "My

shoulder is the last part of my body that I'm thinking about after kissing you."

She smiled briefly. "When did it happen?"

He was quiet a moment, one of those deliberation points. *I was your lover. Talk to me.*

"Back in 2013. On April third. Helmand province."

"Afghanistan? I'm sorry."

He was silent.

She didn't feel like she had the right to push him this time. "I didn't even see a scar the other night." *When you were naked and we were making love.* She wished she wouldn't blush. There was no need to blush. They were adults, both of them.

He smoothed one finger over her flushed cheek. "It was a little too dark for that."

"The interior lights were on for a few minutes, when we were wet." She'd been shivering, wringing out her wet hair, feasting her eyes on a nude man's strong back, his muscular backside. Gosh, she really was blushing. "I can't believe I missed something like a bullet wound."

"I wasn't shot. It was a vehicle rollover. My skin stayed nice and intact, so no scars, but the bones inside shattered a bit. It's not that big of a deal. If I lift my arm too high, my shoulder reminds me not to do that anymore. For the rest of my life." He shook out his left arm again. "It's already stopped hurting."

"I don't believe that."

"It's true. It doesn't hurt."

"I don't believe that's the whole story. People don't remember the date of a simple car accident. It was more than that, wasn't it?" It scared her, to think that he'd lived a life where he could have been killed any day of the year, two different years. How easily they might never have stood on the patio in their prom pose, cheek to cheek.

"Hey," Graham said softly, and she knew her face had given away her thoughts. "Sweet girl. It's okay."

"No, it's really not." She remembered how much he'd wanted to disappear, to go off the grid. It was hard to escape memories.

Whenever you remember Graham and Emily by the lake that night...

She'd given him a good memory, the best, something to balance out the bad. Maybe she could have been the right woman for him.

She'd tried, but she'd failed. She had to leave him tomorrow and go back to Oklahoma. She had no job, no say in where she lived, what she studied, when she'd graduate.

The gelding tried to throw up his head. She shushed him, but she frowned at the halter. "Did you put the halter on this horse?"

One of the metal clips had its latch toward the horse's face. It was a little thing, but she explained that over hours of work, it could irritate the horse. "Like I said, we're all about keeping everything healthy and injury-free around here." She unclipped it, then clipped it on with its curved side toward the horse's face to show Graham how it went. Then she unclipped it, put it on backward again, and stepped back. "Okay, you change it."

Gus chuckled from behind them. "You could have left it the right way."

The foreman's sudden presence startled Emily. Graham didn't care for being sneaked up on, she could tell by the way his jaw clenched a little, but he answered his uncle amiably enough. "She's training me right, and you know it." He unclipped the fastener, turned it the right way.

Gus frowned at her instead of beaming with approval. "Did you choose this gelding for him?"

"Of course not. Sid and Bonner were having themselves a good old time."

Gus sighed. "Well, I'm glad you're here now. Trey wants Graham to start riding. You're the best person I know to train someone on horseback."

Good ol' Emily. She'll work all day because she loves this ranch. Grew up on it, you know.

That mindset was there, so obvious now that she'd seen it. She'd helped start it, unknowingly, as a teenager. It was up to her to stop it, too.

Don't make waves, don't stir things up, play it safe...

The lake had been painfully cold, but she didn't regret that she'd made a splash. She would've only regretted it if she hadn't.

She turned to Gus. "Let me be sure I understand. You want me to spend my day off sharing my experience and using my skill to get your greenhorn started on horsemanship?"

"You don't think Sid or Bonner could do a better job, do you?"

Was that how easily Gus had manipulated her in the past? Just by pitting her in competition with the boys?

"No, I know they can't. But they are on payroll today. You are getting a salary right this minute. *Graham* is getting paid right now. Trey wants him to ride? Trey gets a third of the profits this ranch turns. And yet, I'm being asked to train your new hire for free."

"You love to be with the horses," Gus said, stubborn as the day was long.

Even though there was nothing she'd like more than to spend the day with Graham, Emily was playing the long game now. Everything she did would set the tone for years to come.

"No."

"No?" Gus repeated.

"No, I will not work for free while you two are being paid."

She handed the gelding's lead to Gus and walked away. Her very first step took her past Graham. She heard his quiet chuckle as she passed him.

She was leading her mare out of the stall when she heard Graham tell his uncle he needed the day off.

She was tightening the cinch on her saddle when Gus told Graham he'd get docked a day's pay.

She was putting the bridle over her mare's pretty face when Graham walked up to her. "Now neither one of us is getting paid today. You promised to take me riding the next time I was in town. I did leave town yesterday morning. Got lost for sixty miles and then returned, so this is the next time."

When had her hard bodyguard become charming?

He spoke more quietly, in case Gus was still listening to them. "You said you'd take me for my first ride. That needs to be today, or someone much uglier and more unpleasant than you will do it."

It was tough to return his smile. He'd seen her failure with Gus. She still had to confess her failure with her parents. "This isn't how I imagined it. I thought you'd be done with your three months off the grid. I'd be working here. We'd be together for…well, for more than a day."

"But this is what we have. Keep your promise, sweet girl. Take me riding."

Chapter Seventeen

Graham hadn't realized he'd need to be a horse psychologist to be a good rider. "If your horse got to run a little bit and have some fun, would mine get jealous and try to run, too?"

"It's possible." Emily led the way to one of the shade trees that dotted the landscape. "You might want to dismount, just in case. You can stand with the reins nice and loose. She'll be good. Don't let her get her chest in front of you, though."

Jeez, just standing still with a horse took effort. The whole experience so far had taught Graham how far he had to go just to be passable in the saddle. He wouldn't admit it—ever—but when he'd swung himself up into the saddle for the first time, he'd thought that being on horseback was a hell of a lot farther off the ground than it looked.

He dismounted reasonably gracefully. He looked up at Emily, who had no idea how much she knew. She knew she was good with horses, but she was twenty-two-years good, never having been far from a horse since birth.

"Go ahead," he said. "Show me how it's done. Let's see some speed."

"You want to watch me gallop?"

"Exactly."

"That doesn't sound very fun for you."

She was so very wrong. As he watched her sweeping in a wide arc through the pasture, he felt a very real pleasure. Horse and rider were graceful, beautiful by any standard, but more than that, this was Emily, his Emily, the woman he knew intimately, flying like magic, riding like a stunt-woman, *absolutely spectacular*. Always.

When she came back, she looked down at him from her horse, and he felt a moment of reverence for her. She was amazing. She was better than he could ever deserve.

He wanted his hands on her.

She wanted more than that. They were kissing from the moment she dismounted. Even as she tied her horse next to his, he was kissing the back of her neck, and then she turned into him. Her leather gloves hit the ground at their feet and her warm hands were under his clothes, sliding up his body.

She spoke his name over his lips. She whispered in his ear, "Did you bring protection?"

No—so he needed to slow things down. He kept his hand on the side of her neck, braced his other hand on the tree trunk behind her. "I thought I was spending the day with Sid and Bonner, shoveling out stalls. Not exactly the kind of day you slip a packet in your pocket for."

She panted from their kisses but frowned with concern. "Those two are going to try to trick you. So be careful. They won't give up."

"It's not so different from the military. They feel obligated to try to haze the greenhorn, but they aren't thrilled that I'm the greenhorn. I'm a tougher bite than they ever expected to have to chew, but they'll get me sooner or later. Then they'll be relieved to give it up."

"They'll get you?"

"Of course." He shrugged. "I'll forget to check if the sugar is really salt or something dumb. It'll be over after that. But I'll give them a run for their money first."

Emily started to smile, started to sigh and ended up shaking her head. "I wish I had your confidence."

You did. Where did it go?

The hesitant Emily he was looking at now was too different from the bold Emily who'd kissed him goodbye at dawn yesterday. He'd been with her most of the day yesterday, so he knew she'd been disappointed with Gus. He didn't know how things had gone later. He should have asked sooner.

"How did things go with your parents last night?"

"How did you know I went to see them?"

"I knocked on Trey's door, looking for you. When I saw you this morning in the barn, I assumed they hadn't kicked you out." He ducked his head to see her face better. "Did they?"

Her dark eyes welled with tears. "I'm so... I'm so sorry."

Cursing himself for not seeing the problem sooner, Graham pulled her away from the tree and held her against his chest. "It's going to be okay. If you can't live with Trey, then we'll find a place to live together, somewhere nearby. I have some money." He gave her an encouraging squeeze. "I didn't finish my master's either, remember? We'll spend that."

"Oh, Graham, it's not like that." Her tears were falling now. "I have a place to live. Oklahoma Tech. I have to go back." She wiped her cheeks with her hand. "But I'm not taking any master's courses. I have to take three classes to keep my apartment, so I insisted that I choose the other two. They'll be undergrad classes toward a minor. I'll graduate this May, and that will be the absolute end of it."

She tried to pull away from him. He didn't want to let her go, not while tears were falling. He cupped her head with his hand and held her against his chest.

It took her a long while to relax into his arms, another few minutes after that to stop crying and catch her breath.

He smoothed a few loose strands away from her face. "We're just back to our original plan. Three months apart. Twelve weeks. We can do that."

"But I'm not the woman you thought I was. I was going to be this great rancher, Miss Independent. I was going to finish my degree online this summer. I was going to pay my own way and have my own place to live. I've done none of that. None of it. You have every right to be so... disillusioned. That Emily you made love to? She didn't last long. I failed. I'm so sorry."

"When did you decide all this?"

"Last night, I knew it."

"Why did you want to make love to me under this tree just now? Was that supposed to be break-up sex?"

That sounded pretty bad—and pretty accurate. Since he held her face in his hands, she couldn't hide. "Well..." She bit her lip. "I wanted to feel like I belonged to you just one more time. I'm leaving tomorrow, and you may not be here when I come back for roundup. I'll understand. I wasn't able to make anything work the way I thought it would."

It was stunning that she could think he wouldn't want her because her first run at her goals didn't work out perfectly. This wonderful woman had no idea, none at all, just how wonderful she was.

"Emily, I know you hate the scary military voice, but if you don't adjust your attitude, you're going to hear it."

She sucked in her breath, that little pinprick breath that he already loved.

"You opened up Gus's eyes yesterday. When he said you were overqualified, you called his bluff and accepted the position he'd just said you were qualified for. If Trey hadn't come home, you would have had Gus in a corner. This morning, refusing to work for free was a winning strategy. Gus is going to realize your value quickly.

"Even when it comes to college, you succeeded. You're not going to waste your time or money or effort on master's degree classes you don't want. You did it. You got the main thing you wanted, even if you had to trade September for May.

"I'm in awe of you. I don't want to say you're perfect or you're a goddess, because I don't want you to be that unreachable, but believe me when I say that I know I'm reaching above myself to be with you. You are everything exciting in the world. You have a future. You have the daring to go after happiness. Watching you strip by a pond, watching you gallop your horse, watching you braid your hair—you bring me to my knees, Emily. To my knees."

He held her face in his hands and kissed her cheeks, her nose, her forehead. "So you go ahead and have your doubts. You go ahead and keep trying to get better. That's you going after the future you want. But while you're in the middle of making your dreams a reality, you need to know that when I kiss you, I already taste that bit of perfection that is you."

If she wanted to belong to him one more time, then he was willing to oblige. He could do it without that damned foil packet. He kissed her face, her throat. He bent his head and kissed her breast through the warm plaid of her shirt, and then he dropped to one knee. He put his arms around her waist and pressed the side of his face to her stomach. Then he was on both knees, undoing her belt, anticipating that bit of perfection.

Emily put her hands in his hair for balance. "Graham, what are you doing?"

But of course, she already knew.

He smiled anyway and told her. "I'm belonging to you."

Ten weeks down, two to go.

Graham rode his horse into the temporary camp, counting the days. The James Hill Ranch would begin its roundup two weeks from now, and Emily would come home for nine days on her spring break. The days would be hard and they would be long, but they'd be spent side by side with the woman he missed so much. His heart hurt with the sheer anticipation of it.

Before the roundup of the thousands of calves on the James Hill, he'd get his first taste of the work today at this smaller, neighboring ranch. The Chavez family was known for having the first roundup of the spring, and they threw a picnic for everyone who came to help. A wood fire was already smoking meat by an old-fashioned chuck wagon. Then roundups would begin at other ranches, one after the other. The James Hill would be the biggest one in two weeks, and the River Mack would be the last one in May.

Graham knew the basic concept. All the calves that had been born in the spring were required by law to be branded, doctored, tagged and counted. Most of the ranching in January and February had centered on putting out hay bales and other tame stuff, but roundup was the real deal, with the cattle herded into a fenced area by the hundreds, bawling and dusty. Cowboys on horseback rode among them, lassos at the ready, scattering the cattle as they looked for unbranded calves. The men threw their lassos at running calves while on running horses themselves.

How long is that going to take me to learn?

Ranching was nothing if not humbling.

Graham enjoyed it, though. There was the same sense of camaraderie he'd once felt in a platoon, minus the threat of violence. Wrestling a cow to wash out an infected eye required as much teamwork as clearing an enemy bunker. Repairing fence lines had been as much a test of strength and grit as a road march wearing sixty-five pounds of war gear. The edgy sense of alertness that had never quite left Graham served a purpose once more, but rather than looking for things that might kill him, he was looking for things to fix, animals to help, weather to prepare for.

Luke and Trey had offered him a six-month contract yesterday, and since Graham couldn't imagine going back to suits and ties, he'd taken it. From what he'd seen so far this morning, he was going to need all six months to get proficient with a lasso. He stood at the fence with members of the Chavez family to watch and learn.

Each calf was roped by either the head or the back leg—heading or heeling—and the horses would back up immediately to keep the ropes taut. Other cowboys on foot then ran in to lay the calf on its side. The calf was branded and doctored, then released from the ropes and allowed to trot back to the milling herd. Each calf was on the ground for less than a minute, a point of pride among the cowboys. The Chavezes' herd of hundreds would be done in one day.

Graham couldn't watch the roping without thinking of Emily and her rodeo event. Then he couldn't watch the roping because he was expected to give each calf a dose of medicine, working as part of the James Hill team as they took their turn to earn their supper.

Luke and Trey manhandled the calves. There was a technique to it. When the calves were caught by the heel, they could be laid down pretty easily by using their tail and a leg. The ones caught by the head were more difficult, needing to be picked up completely off their feet and thumped onto their sides. That was hundreds of pounds of protesting, kicking beef that had to be manhandled. Obviously, everyone preferred the calves to be heeled.

Sid and Bonner were on a streak. Ten consecutive calves had been brought to the branding irons by the head.

"For the love of God, can't you heel one?" Everyone had been razzing them for heading all the calves, but Luke was starting to get ticked off. He looked around the crowd of neighborhood cowboys milling at the fence. "Emily! Come save our backs. Sid, get out of there. Let Emily handle it."

Emily. Graham turned to look, and sure enough, there was the woman he loved, sitting on a horse she loved, wearing a braid down her back. She looked amazing in full color, vivid 3-D after a ten-week absence—not twelve. Had he ever said he didn't want her to be an untouchable goddess? Too bad. She was a goddess on horseback.

Trey slapped him on the back. "She just got in an hour ago. You're supposed to be surprised."

"I am." Not once during all their phone calls and video chats had she hinted that she'd be home today.

Luke took off his hat and smacked it against his chaps to get the dust off. "Watch this. She gets it from me. I taught her everything she knows."

Graham watched. Emily might as well have been a centaur, she moved so fluidly with the horse as it cut in every direction, but it was her roping that thrilled the crowd. Within a minute, she rode over to them with her first calf, both of its back legs neatly caught in her lasso, making everyone else's job easier. Everyone on the ground professed their love for her, but Graham meant it.

He was going to marry her.

Emily stood before the main building on campus and posed for photos in her cap and gown with each person who had made the trip to her graduation. Her mother smoothed her stole and centered her *summa cum laude* gold cord at least every third shot.

It was humbling how many people cared enough to make the long drive to Oklahoma. Her parents, grandparents, sisters and brother-in-law, Aunt Jessie and Uncle James, Trey and his fiancée, Luke and his wife were here, and Gus, who still claimed to be prettier than she was.

And, of course, Benjamin Graham, who slayed her with a wink when nobody was looking. They had a secret.

Everyone knew they were going to get married this year, and everyone knew that Graham had gotten her the best graduation gift a girl could want: cattle. The fifty thousand dollars he'd saved by not completing his master's degree had purchased fifty head of a rare breed of cattle, one intended for a specialty market. The land for them to graze on was unaffordable, but the James Hill Ranch would allow her herd to graze there in return for half the calves born the first year.

Emily and Graham had designed and registered their own brand. They'd both be working the entire herd at the James Hill, but from now on, at roundup and when moving cattle to auction, she and Graham were going to have to be on their best horses to cut their cattle out of the James Hill herd. She looked forward to it. She was a cattle rancher.

"Okay, everyone," her mother called. "Let's head over to the restaurant. It's time for the party."

Graham came up behind Emily and put his arms around her. Prom pose, cap and gown version. "You ready?"

"You bet."

They waited until the rest of the group had cleared out, and then Emily took off her square cap. Her long hair flowed freely down her back, almost to her waist. She shed her graduation robe. Underneath, she wore a mini dress, one with bright, white ruffles up to her neck.

She and Graham just had one stop to make before they met everyone at the restaurant. Her mother didn't know it yet, but Emily's graduation party was about to become a wedding reception.

"This is going to be so fun." Emily slid her fingers between Graham's, and they ran all the way to the courthouse.

* * * * *

And don't miss out on previous books in the
TEXAS RESCUE *series:*

A COWBOY'S WISH UPON A STAR
HER TEXAS RESCUE DOCTOR
FOLLOWING DOCTOR'S ORDERS
A TEXAS RESCUE CHRISTMAS

Available now from Mills & Boon Cherish!

Acknowledgments

I received much-needed support to complete this book, so I really must thank:

Gail Chasan, for being so encouraging while keeping one eye on the clock for me so that I didn't have to worry. Much.

My husband, for five pans of enchiladas, fifty you-can-do-it-honeys, and a thousand real-life kisses to help me write one fictional kiss.

Sam Hunt, for keeping me company all night long, one writing session after another, *just us and the speakers on.*

MILLS & BOON®

Cherish™

EXPERIENCE THE ULTIMATE RUSH OF FALLING IN LOVE

A sneak peek at next month's titles...

In stores from 10th August 2017:

- **Sarah and the Secret Sheikh** – Michelle Douglas *and* **Romancing the Wallflower** – Michelle Major
- **A Proposal from the Crown Prince** – Jessica Gilmore *and* **A Wedding to Remember** – Joanna Sims

In stores from 24th August 2017:

- **Her New York Billionaire** – Andrea Bolter *and* **The Waitress's Secret** – Kathy Douglass
- **Conveniently Engaged to the Boss** – Ellie Darkins *and* **The Maverick's Bride-to-Order** – Stella Bagwell

---

Just can't wait?
Buy our books online before they hit the shops!
www.millsandboon.co.uk

Also available as eBooks.

MILLS & BOON®

EXCLUSIVE EXTRACT

Artist Holly Motta arrives in New York to find billionaire Ethan Benton in the apartment where *she's* meant to be staying! And the next surprise? Ethan needs a fake fiancée and he wants *her* for the role…

Read on for a sneak preview of
HER NEW YORK BILLIONAIRE
by debut author Andrea Bolter

"In exchange for you posing as my fiancée, as I have outlined, you will be financially compensated and you will become legal owner of this apartment and any items such as clothes and jewels that have been purchased for this position. Your brother's career will not be impacted negatively should our work together come to an end. *And…*" He paused for emphasis.

Holly leaned forward in her chair, her back still board-straight.

"I have a five-building development under construction in Chelsea. There will be furnished apartments, office lofts and common space lobbies – all in need of artwork. I will commission you for the project."

Holly's lungs emptied. A commission for a big corporate project. That was exactly what she'd hoped she'd find in New York. A chance to have her work seen by thousands of people. The kind of exposure that could lead from one job to the next and to a sustained and successful career.

This was all too much. Fantastic, frightening, impossible… Obviously getting involved in any way with Ethan Benton was a terrible idea. She'd be beholden to him. Serving another person's agenda again. Just what she'd come to New York to get away from.

But this could be a once-in-a-lifetime opportunity. An apartment. A job. It sounded as if he was open to most any demand she could come up with. She really did owe it to herself to contemplate this opportunity.

Her brain was no longer operating normally. The clock on Ethan's desk reminded her that it was after midnight. She'd left Fort Pierce early that morning.

"That really is an incredible offer…" She exhaled. "But I'm too tired to think straight. I'm going to need to sleep on it."

"As you wish."

Holly moved to collect the luggage she'd arrived with. Ethan beat her to it and hoisted the duffle bag over his shoulder. He wrenched the handle of the suitcase. Its wheels tottered as fast as her mind whirled as she followed him to the bedroom.

"Goodnight, then." He placed the bags just inside the doorway and couldn't get out of the room fast enough.

Before closing the door she poked her head out and called, "Ethan Benton, you don't play fair."

Over his shoulder, he turned his face back toward her. "I told you. I always get what I want."